What It Might Feel Like to Hope

"Dorene O'Brien's stories operate on a different plane and dimension of realism–flesh and blood yet dipped in a neon wash . . . O'Brien's prose possesses a particular cinema that will not just stay in your mind but your gut as well."

– Porochista Khakpour, author of *Sick*

"Like all superb constructions, Dorene O'Brien's magical new collection of short fiction, *What It Might Feel Like to Hope*, quickly transports readers beyond the bones of its structure—the deftly crafted plots, striking characterizations and clever, lyrical prose—to places of genuine wonder."

– Laura Bernstein-Machlay, author of *Travelers*

"A panoply of humanity—characters who are hilarious and real and bumble through life making the same mistakes as the rest of us."

– Kelly Fordon, author of *Garden for the Blind*

These stories "remind us what it means to be human and the myriad ways we work out its complexities."

– Lolita Hernandez, author of *Autopsy of an Engine*

What It Might Feel Like to Hope "takes readers on a wondrous journey that is at times laugh-out-loud humorous, at times heartbreaking, but always compelling and magnificent in its authenticity . . . the thread of hope—in all its desperate and wonderful glory—weaves its magic throughout this gem."

– Ksenia Rychtycka, author of *Crossing the Border*

"Entering closely and powerfully into the varied lives of her concisely drawn characters, O'Brien shows an uncommon sympathy to the struggling, the beleaguered, even the obtuse and the angry. In doing so, she brings to us humor, tenderness and, yes, hope."

– Sarah Shoemaker, author of *Mr. Rochester*

"What gives these fine stories real heft is their authenticity, which O'Brien achieves through masterful use of voice, dialogue, and accurate detail. You trust her storytelling utterly."

– José Skinner, author of *The Tombstone Race*

"O'Brien links her stories not with the traditional steel of recurring characters or connected plotlines, but with the silken thread of shared desires, destinies, and the refusal to relinquish either to the quotidian challenges of circumstance."

– Laura Hulthen Thomas, author of *States of Motion*

"O'Brien's collection of stories takes us on a wild ride from [the] seemingly mundane . . . to the depths of sorrow."

– Anca Vlasopolos, author of *Cartographies of Scale (and Wing)*

"The stories in Dorene O'Brien's *What It Might Feel Like to Hope* are heartbreaking, funny, thoughtful and keenly attuned to the frailties of humans and their often ineffectual attempts to connect with each other. . . . Deliciously all over the place, yet tight and cohesive, once these stories drop their truth bombs, you're left both dazed and sated by their richness."

– Michael Zadoorian, author of *Beautiful Music*

WHAT IT MIGHT FEEL LIKE TO HOPE

WHAT IT MIGHT FEEL LIKE TO HOPE

stories

DORENE O'BRIEN

BAOBAB PRESS
RENO, NV

Selected stories in this work previously appeared in earlier forms in the following magazines and journals: "Eight Blind Dates Later" in *Baltimore Review*; "Turn of the Wind" in *Ars Medica*; "Honesty Above All Else" in *Detroit Noir*; "Reaping" in *Peregrine*; "Tom Hanks Wants a Story" in *Madison Review*; "What It Might Feel Like to Hope" in *The Republic of Letters*; "Little Birds" in *Red Rock Review*; "A Short Distance Behind Us" in *Montreal Review*; "Pocket Philosophers" in *Prick of the Spindle* (Special Kindle edition); and "Harm None" in *Driftwood*.

First Printing

ISBN-13: 978-1-936097-21-0
ISBN-10: 1-936097-21-4

Library of Congress Control Number: 2018950307

Baobab Press
121 California Avenue
Reno, Nevada 89509
www.baobabpress.com

Printed in the United States

For always giving me hope,
this book is dedicated to Pat, Hadley and Chloe

contents

WHAT IT MIGHT FEEL LIKE TO HOPE

eight blind dates later

I was drunk and lonely and tired of Googling my name only to find a high school drama teacher in the throes of a failing *Pippin* production, a fat bastard who brews his own beer, and a host of other Johnny Danes who by comparison should have made me feel celebratory but instead only darkened my mood. I moved on, and that's when I found her website, when I had exhausted myself with searches of football scores, '62 Impalas and Johnny Danes. She soared into my head the way she had soared into my dreams so many times before, uninvited and unwelcome. Of course she looked good. Who puts an ugly picture of herself on a website? She was now writing bodice rippers, their covers a lurid blur across my flickering screen, a collage of tint, lace, and skin. There it was, another bullet on my growing list of disgraces: I had been dumped by a romance novelist.

So there I sat, reading about Cyril and Morgan, Devon and Lord Stoke. "His face hardened impossibly. 'Aye, ye tempt me, Brianna. I think aboot succumbing tae ma lust an' usin' yer pretty body.'" This one had a Scottish vibe, women running across moors from supermen going commando in kilts. Closer inspection revealed that all of her books, apparently written in a matter of months, had a theme. The cover of *Matrimonial Merger* features stockbroker Jefferson Steele and his voluptuous bespectacled secretary Reena reaching toward each other across a mahogany desk, folders, pens and other office paraphernalia captured in mid-flight after having been pushed off by greedy, impatient hands. The excerpt read, "She touched his beefy chest, slid her hand down the front of his $300 Brooks Brothers dress trousers. 'Looks like the stock market is *up*,' she purred."

Wild Card is about Jack, a handsome card sharp with unnaturally large biceps, and Keira, the casino owner's daughter, a dark-eyed brunette who for some reason has playing cards spilling from her cleavage as she turns from his embrace. I tried to predict what the excerpt would say as I shuffled to the kitchen for another beer: "Jack stared at Keira's bosom for a moment before saying, 'That's quite a pair'" or "Keira slid her tongue across Jack's throbbing abs and said, 'Don't worry, I'll raise you.'"

I MET SHELBY WHEN SHE brought her car into Merrick Chrysler where I manage the body shop. Normally I don't pay much attention to traffic in the garage, but I heard her car before I even saw it. It was a new Sebring, its front and back so far out of alignment they should have been on separate vehicles. The metal, twisted beyond even my comprehension, groaned as she slowly wheeled into the fifth bay. Everyone in the shop turned and stared as she clacked toward the intake station in her too-tall heels, one of which promptly caught in a drainage grate, tipping her forward onto the oil-stained concrete.

"Easy," I said, not to her but as a warning to the porters—a couple of high school punks who spent their lunch hours smoking weed out back–not to let her see them laughing. I helped her up, and what amazed me most was that she wasn't the least bit embarrassed, a trait, I now realize, not uncommon in romance writers. She said that she had locked her brakes on I-84 after looking up to see a jackknifed semi before her, sending her car into three spins before it settled neatly against the median. Who doesn't notice a flipped semi on the freeway in front of them?

She asked if I could fix the car and I scratched my head because I was confounded not only by the car—how had she driven it from the accident site to the dealership?—but by her. "How long will it take?" she chirped.

"Well," I said, "we're going to have to look at that frame, see if we can get it on a straightener—"

"Will it be done today?" She smiled. "I have a blind date tonight!"

This was Shelby, a woman who could not see a crisis if it slammed her in the head and then rode over her. A fire in the kitchen? We'll eat out! A sick friend? I'll donate a kidney! An earthquake? I'll get a broom! I was drawn to her immediately, her confidence, her cheerfulness, her limping around her mangled car with a broken heel, pointing out the obvious: *This door won't shut! This wheel is bent! It's all crooked!* She was unlike the other women I had dated, whose dispositions collectively suggested that the world had offended them in extreme and unforgivable ways. I offered to drive her home, I made her vehicle a top priority, I even gave her a box of tree-shaped car fresheners. Who had I become? For the first time in my life, an optimist. To the dismay of my mechanics, I demanded they put the lopsided Sebring on the straightener and pull that little car like taffy. This was no small task as the car seemed to have taken to its deformity and put up a damn good fight.

I asked her out to dinner that very night, surely a poor substitute for her blind date, one I would work to keep her from rescheduling. Sure, I'd just been dumped by the latest in a long line of girlfriends who had ultimately found that I was either too boring or too distant, which when you think about it is really the same thing. But Shelby's optimism, viewed against the darkly brooding women I'd recently dated, was attractive, contagious even. So we went to Joe's Crab Shack and watched apathetic teens sing uninspired versions of "Happy Birthday" to tables of screaming kids and senior citizens who looked by turns confused and ecstatic. Then I drove her home to an apartment building about three miles from my house, the Garden Arms, which, from what I could tell, had neither.

"This was really nice of you," she said.

"Well, I had to eat."

"Still."

"Maybe I could pick you up in the morning, drive you to work."

"Oh," she said before staring at me as if looking at my face long enough would reveal whether I was a serial killer. Finally, she asked for my number. "Can I call you later and let you know?"

"Not a problem," I said.

She did call that night, and the night after and the night after that. For the next week I drove her to At a Fast Clip where she bleached hair and cut bangs and generally made women happy for what remained of their day. When her car was ready I didn't tell her, instead making up stories about a faulty part or a failed alignment test. Sure, I was starting to like her, even if she was short and about ten pounds over the red line on the imaginary scale in my head. She was perky and consistently interested in everything I said.

Before long Shelby and I were inseparable, spurring each other on to new heights of buoyancy. The mechanics eyed me suspiciously as they chewed on the donuts I brought to work each morning, and my mother was convinced I'd been diagnosed with a terminal disease when I started calling her twice a week to inquire about her bunions. My friends stopped inviting me for beers when I proved to be too cheerful in the face of their personal calamities: nagging wives, spiteful bosses, ungrateful kids. I didn't care; I had Shelby, my mainline to euphoria. If someone had told me that I would one day be reading my ex-girlfriend's romance trash on the Internet, I would have clapped him on the back and bet my life savings he was wrong.

But there I was, staring through the saloon doors spanning the cover of *Three on a Stallion*, which featured a bosomy, befeathered redhead posed between a half-dressed cowboy and a Boss Hogg type replete with bolo tie and gold-encrusted pinkie ring. *Where's the horse?* I wondered.

The double meaning of *No Man's Land* was not lost on me: a defiant blond in full camo, hands on hips, looking haughty and disinterested as men dressed in sailor suits, dress blues, olive drabs, Flak jackets and riot gear gaze from a confusing collage of desert, ocean and sky in the background. The tagline for this one read, "It had been years since a man had crossed Terra's border and that's just the way she liked it. That is, until Malkham invaded."

I tried to read some of the excerpts on her site, but when I saw the words "Tanner pulled the coverlet down to reveal Ciara's shapely legs, his eyes tracing their curves up toward her womanhood," I slammed down the last of my Bud and stumbled into bed. I didn't dream of her, but if I had it would have gone something like this: Shelby glaring at me, disappointment spilling from her pores before the machete in her hand cleaves off my penis. You don't need a Freudian therapist to unravel that.

When I went to my mother's the next day she accosted me before I had even removed my jacket. "I have a thought," she bellowed.

"What's up?" I asked as I plopped onto a kitchen chair, resigned to cold rigatoni and an unfailing exuberance that was hard to bear without Shelby beside me, smiling, encouraging my mother to share bodily emission updates, coupon-savings totals, the escapades of Mr. Bojangles, a flea-bitten, imperious cat that seemed intent on disfiguring my face.

"You remember Mrs. Candello?"

I searched my memory banks, knowing it was entirely possible that she did not exist there. Lately my mother has grown forgetful, repeating the same stories, misplacing her thyroid pills, believing that our shared history is so entwined that our list of acquaintances must be identical. "No," I said, "can't say that I do."

"From the grocery store?"

I shook my head.

"Bingo?"

This went on for several minutes until I deduced that Mrs. Candello had a daughter near my age who was in dire need of a date.

"Mom, I don't want to go on a date."

"Well, of course you do!"

I shook my head. "Give me one good reason."

"I can give you plenty!"

I stared at the chipped plate on the table before me, the paper napkin folded neatly under a child-sized fork, the paisley pattern in the plastic tablecloth. When our eyes met, her look carried the weight of her disappointment in my selfishness and the gross injustice to poor Alice Candello, a nice girl with a tiny overbite who daily underwent the strain of fielding telephone complaints from angry AT&T customers.

"Do you know how difficult that is, dealing with irritated people? The woman's a saint. You're too good to have a cup of coffee with a saint?"

"I'm sure she's great," I said, exhausted before I put the first bite of cold, wet noodle into my mouth. "But I don't want to start anything–"

"She's not asking for a marriage proposal. Just a cup of coffee. Maybe she won't even like you," she said almost hopefully before placing a warm glass of RC Cola beside my hand and lowering herself onto the chair next to me.

"I'm sure she won't."

"Oh, Johnny, you've been so negative since . . ."

"Since what?"

She ignored my question, serving herself a congealed mass of pasta with exaggerated concentration while patting Mr. Bojangles, who seemed to have materialized from her outstretched hand before regarding me with steely eyes.

"Since what?" I persisted.

"Since what *what*?"

"I've been so negative since what?"

She shook her head as if having a silent argument with an invisible antagonist. "Since you and Shelby broke up," she blurted. "She was such a nice girl."

"She was—is—a nice girl. I just wasn't ready for, you know." I swirled my fork in the air. "Anything."

Her eyebrows and nose seemed to reach for one another and I imagined the rusted cogs in the wheels of her mind working to produce meaning. I placed my hand over hers. "I appreciate that you're doing something nice for me. I appreciate that you want me to be happy."

"I don't know why Shelby didn't make you happy. She made *me* happy."

After cleaning up the kitchen I drove home through the snow-bound streets and thought about Shelby, whose mother probably did not need to engage the heroic extremes mine did to launch her child on a date. I stared at the passenger seat from where Shelby had once snorted iced tea onto the windshield after I told a moderately funny joke, where she once winked so hard her contact lens sprung from her eye, where for weeks after our breakup the indents of her butt cheeks remained outlined in the leather cushion.

It had been a year since I told Shelby that moving clothes into my closet without permission, choosing engagement rings without my knowledge, and leaving copies of *Brides* magazine on my coffee table were undermining her desired outcome. I should have known what I was up against when she started sleeping at my place more often than her own, cooking my favorite meals, and asking how many kids I wanted. We were in our late twenties and had only been dating for six months. Six months! She told me, ironically, that time didn't matter when you were in love but that she was ready *now*.

Painful though it may be, human nature drives us to tongue the crater left by a pulled tooth, save the collars of deceased pets, troll the websites of former lovers. I was curious to know if Shelby was in a relationship or if she was so devastated by our breakup that she'd sworn off men entirely. When I clicked on her site, the screen exploded in green and red, the cover of a holiday-themed book called *He Was Naughty, She Was Nice* featuring a teary-eyed, Christmas sweater-clad blond clinched in the embrace of a shirtless torso—apparently the reader could crown the body with the face of her own personal villain. They are outside in the snow. At night. Under a mistletoe-laden pine tree. Maybe this is brilliant. What do

I know? But a Christmas sweater? Shirtless in freezing temps? Why so many mistletoes? The tagline: "This Christmas, Holly would *not* be the gift that kept on giving." I tooled around the site until I located the Author Bio, which was a strange blend of personal and professional information: *Originally from Bad Axe, Michigan, Ms. Duchene now lives in Boise, Idaho, with her one-eyed dog, Mabel. She has written six romance novels by night. By day she is a hair stylist. "Be careful," she warns her customers, "or you'll end up in my book!"* Would her bio even mention a significant other? I clicked on the Contact Author link and stared at the online form, which of course required I leave an email address for her response. I left the site and then did what any normal, red-blooded American man would do: I paid $12.95 on Amazon for a paperback romance written by a former girlfriend now living with a one-eyed dog.

Exhausted, I slapped down the lid of the laptop and searched the refrigerator for anything edible. As the lump of leftover rigatoni rotated in the microwave I stared through the kitchen window. The snow was falling softly outside, my mother was on a weekend trip with her neighbor to Amish country, and I did not have to work for the next two days. Life's small gifts should not be minimized. As I watched *Rear Window* on TMC I developed a new appreciation for the characters and the storyline, all this voyeurism and obsession and eroticism delivered without one awkward line.

The next day I selected a small fir from the church parking lot where Ned Pearson had set up a miniature forest from his tree farm. Last year Shelby insisted we buy the biggest pine on the lot only to come home and cut it in half to get it through the front door. Once it was vertical she shook out a tree skirt—where had that come from?—and hummed "Let It Snow" as she worked the quilted material around the metal stand. Under the tree the next morning were seven packages of various shapes and sizes, wrapped in shimmering paper and adorned with handmade paper bows, all addressed to me. Were they hidden in a closet? Had she snuck them from her car while I slept? I was simultaneously thrilled and annoyed, and I considered secretly opening them to determine her investment so that I could reciprocate, but I knew I would never be able to restore the presents to their pristine condition. Instead, I asked what she would like for Christmas, and she cocked her head, smiled and said, "Oh, Johnny, you know what I want!"

I didn't. I bought her seven gifts: a crock pot, a pair of Magic Scissors, a battery-operated candle, a bottle of White Diamonds, a digital pedometer, a Target gift card, and a fiber optic holiday sweater. She looked less than pleased with all of the gifts but the sweater, which she wore later that day to dinner at my mother's. My presents included a pair of Hugo Boss leather gloves, a digital camera, an iPod docking station, a fist-sized chocolate heart, custom car mats, a hand-knit scarf, and a ring.

I SAT ACROSS THE TABLE from Alice Candello at Fin–dark wood, musty smell, overpriced seafood–and learned that she is, indeed, stressed, as evidenced by the crescent-shaped stains under the arms of her satin blouse and the speed with which she downed a $42 bottle of merlot. She did not stop talking—about implacable customers, her obstinate cockatiel, traffic on I-84 where, I could not prevent the thought, Shelby had once spun her car like a carnival ride. The handcuff-sized bangles on her wrist clanked each time she lifted her glass or waved to the waiter to ask for more bread, to request a less tart salad dressing, to demand he open a window as she fanned herself with the cocktail menu. After her fourth glass of wine she'd thrown off any pretense of being on a first date, openly flirting while grinding what felt like a size 18 gumboot up and down my left shin and engaging in a strange dialect of drunken baby talk. I am not an easily embarrassed man, but she was making a Herculean effort, even if unconsciously. By the time the main course arrived, I was mentally rehearsing what I would say to my crestfallen mother: I'm being transferred to Parma, I'm allergic to birds, I'm gay.

But the utter failure of my date with Alice Candello did not deter my perpetually upbeat mother, who apparently had a slew of friends with desperate, defective daughters: recently divorced LuAnn Plug spent the evening chatting about the myriad ways she'd like her ex to suffer (stoning, overpass collapse, shark attack), Stacy Kaminski barely spoke, instead giggling like a mental patient, and Renee Dubois anxiously glanced around the restaurant like a witness protection inductee on her first outing before admitting that her former boyfriend was a stalker but, really, she said, that didn't stop him from loving her.

There's no other way to say it: my mailman is an asshole. Two days after my ill-fated date with a woman who mistook tracking devices and night-vision goggles for the accoutrements of love, I stood at the curb in a knee-high snowdrift left by the plow and worked a large, tightly fused clump of flyers, bills, and a padded envelope from my mailbox. Shelby's book. I threw a frozen pizza into the oven, cracked a beer, and exhumed the paperback from its plastic sheath. The colors on its cover were even brighter, the sweater tackier and the scene more bizarre than they had appeared on her website, but that didn't matter. I found myself attempting to satisfy a curiosity I could not name: Did Shelby have literary talent? Had writing these novels changed her? Had I made a mistake in letting her go? As far as literary talent, how hard can it be to write a romance? But maybe spending time with desperate female characters had opened her eyes to their, well, desperation.

I smiled as I read about Holly, who could have been Shelby herself, or at least the person Shelby saw herself to be: selfless, positive, spirited, unappreciated. Holly even looked like Shelby: short, blond, freckle-faced, snub-nosed, cute. If you're wondering, as I was, her boyfriend Nick looked nothing like me: square-jawed, muscled, stylish but with an incurable propensity for removing his shirt. I already hated him. Nick stood Holly up, broke promises, flirted with other women while Holly made meals, scheduled events and booked trips for a man who cancelled or ignored her. Why? I wondered. Why did Holly put up with him? Maybe women did not give up on men as easily as men did women. Maybe women read romance novels because they understood the general hopelessness of men, commiserated with the dejected heroines. Maybe that's why LuAnn Plug imagined her ex plummeting to his death from a fiery helicopter or running headlong into razor wire. All that effort wasted. All that hope shattered. But I never did that to Shelby. Or at least not to the extent outlined in her book.

I read well into the night. When Holly finally releases Nick—who actually runs off to Europe with Margeaux, leaving her no choice, really—she meets Kris, a kind, bespectacled, stable man who owns a toy factory. Her life is now "constant" and "content." She wears her favorite Christmas sweater to a holiday dinner with Kris's mother, who flits around the kitchen like an epileptic comet and squeals with delight when she opens a Christmas sweater for her cat, Mr. Bojangles. I laughed aloud, imagining both the slashing I would face if I advanced on the real Mr. Bojangles with a sweater and Shelby including me—or something related to me—in her book. Clearly I was on her mind as she wrote her holiday romance. I put the book aside for a while to savor the warmth of being remembered, the memory of being happy.

Meanwhile my mother persisted in battling my resolve, determined to whittle her list of prospective daughters-in-law to zero; when she engaged her exaggerated limp, clutched Mr. Bojangles to her bosom and claimed that she was not long for this world, I acquiesced. While Mona Lambers rambled on about cross-stitch patterns I wondered if Holly would take Nick back; when Loreen Womack ran to the restroom for the fifth time—*Bladder infection*? *Coke addiction*?—I wondered if Nick would or could change. As Patrice Dombrowski chucked oysters into her mouth like an eating-contest contender I hoped that, ultimately, Holly/Shelby would be happy.

The book sat, untouched, on the coffee table like a talisman, like a spell, like an unfulfilled wish. Finally, after a particularly bad day at work—the porters never returned from lunch, one of my mechanics cracked the windshield on a year-old Town & Country with a dropped wrench, an unsatisfied customer threatened to shove his boot so far up my ass I'd taste leather—I decided to reembark on my reading odyssey in an effort to mine some sort of hope from *He Was Naughty, She Was Nice*. The next scene described a holiday party—five pages of partridge-adorned wreaths, candle-laden mantels, the aromatic properties of pine—after which Holly, Heylei, and Anastasia engage in a three-page discussion of the gifts they received from their boyfriends: Tiffany earrings, Pandora charms, Gucci clutches, spa days, trips to Bermuda, engagement rings. I did not take this personally.

Apparently no romance would be complete without *revenge*; the cad must not only lose the girl but must be made the fool, must come to his senses only to realize his transformation—real or imagined—has been futile, for the woman he is now determined to win back has found happiness in the arms of a man who is both lesser and greater, paunchy and cerebral but also generous and kind. By the time Nick bursts through the garland-strangled front door wearing the green and red sequined sweater Holly had made for him, the reader not only anticipates but savors the knowledge that his punishment will be both severe and satisfying. The room collectively sniggers as Nick approaches Holly, shyly proffering a basket of unwrapped gifts, which include a crock pot, a pair of Magic Scissors, a battery-operated candle, a bottle of White Diamonds, a digital pedometer, and a Target gift card. *That* I took personally.

I put down the book and picked up Sheila Kravitz with a newfound will to see the best in people, suppressing my curiosity about why these women were single (after all, I was single, though that was the result of vigilance and resolve). I ignored Sheila's eye tic. I overlooked the force with which her man hands clutched the fork and knife, sawing like a primate into the bloody steak on her plate. I even managed a smile when she made it clear that she was an old-fashioned girl and not amenable to "roving paws." Then I went home, opened a free Gmail account under the pseudonym Clint Harris and launched an email at Shelby through her website:

Dear Ms. Duchene,

I really enjoyed your most recent book, He Was Naughty, She Was Nice. You are a talented writer. I liked the descriptions of the meals, the holiday décor, and the characters. I was wondering how you come up with ideas for your books? Are they pure fiction or do you base your work on people you know? Thanks and keep writing!

Sincerely,

Clint Harris

Shelby's response was almost immediate:

Dear Clint (I hope I can call you Clint!):

Thank you for your kind words. Christmas is one of my favorite holidays so writing the descriptions was fun! Many of them were obtained as I drove around looking at decorations while listening to Christmas carols.

I felt something between a pang and a jolt then, recalling last year when Shelby and I tooled around the neighborhood with a thermos of hot chocolate listening to Bing Crosby and Mannheim Steamroller songs and taking in the rooftop Santas, outsized manger animals, high-voltage light displays. I teased her but had to admit that the over-the-top exhibits and booming music had made me smile. I read on:

Much of what I write is made up, or fictional, though sometimes I will model an event after a real-life experience or a character after someone I know. I hope that answers your question! Please check back for publication information on my next book, Urban Safari: Hunting the Two-Legged Beast.

Happy reading!

Shelby

I replied of course:

Thanks for your quick response. Being as I am a man, I was wondering how men feel about your insights into the male psyche. For example, I think you were spot on in that a jerk like Nick does not deserve Holly and that he should be punished—maybe he will even learn a lesson about how to treat women. But I was wondering what was so horrible about, say, a gift of perfume or a gift card or even a pedometer in the current health-conscious craze. Again, just curious!

Thanks,
Clint

I waited until, as a writer might say, the sun fell into the far-off hills and the stars filled the sky and I grew tired. The next morning, I checked my Gmail before work and found only an Olga's coupon, a GoFundMe request and a loan consolidation offer. All day at work, as I greeted customers, calculated estimates, and kept loose tabs on the porters, I wondered if Shelby had figured out it was me. I thought I did a good job of masking my identity, but maybe she understood the complex workings of the web in a way that I never would, somehow following the string of my fake name and account back to me. My paranoia dissolved when I saw her response later that evening.

Dear Clint:

While I know that more women than men read my books (and romances in general), I do think lots of men read them and understand that certain behaviors are unacceptable. The presents listed in the book are fine for, say, your aunt or your mother or even someone who requests those gifts specifically. But when Nick offers Shelby those gifts, he reveals that he has not considered who she is and what she needs from him. Generic merchandise will not please her (or any girlfriend, especially one he is hoping to win back). Hope that answers your questions!

All the Best,
Shelby

But when Nick offers *Shelby* those gifts? Was that a Freudian slip, a revelation that Holly is Shelby's alter ego and Nick is me, or at least a symbol of my thoughtlessness? I finished the book that night, though of course the ending was predictable: the party guests openly mock Nick's pathetic attempt at reconciliation, and after he is physically thrown from the house he stares through the front window as Kris bends to one knee, pulls a black velvet box from his pocket and looks hopefully up at Shelby/Holly. I threw the book across the room while simultaneously wondering if Alice Candello might be more palatable if she laid off the wine.

The next day I decided that I would have dinner with my best girl: Mom. I bought the fixings for her favorite meal: chicken, green peppers, onions, tomatoes, garlic, white wine for the crock pot cacciatore accompanied by baby potatoes smothered in butter and finished off with a dessert of chocolate ice cream. Though she had been the author of the torment I had endured on numerous blind dates, she'd always had the best intentions. When she arrived, I greeted her at the front door and took her coat. "Right this way, Madam," I said and offered my arm.

"My," she exclaimed, "all those dates turned you into a gentleman!"

"I was always a gentleman," I protested.

"Yes, but you're nice again!"

I was trying. She sat down in the living room as I trotted to the kitchen to check on the potatoes and fetch the remainder of the wine I'd used in the recipe, and when I returned my mother was bent over, pulling something from under the sofa. Shelby's book.

"What's this?"

"A poorly written book," I said, reaching for it, but she just stared at it, mesmerized.

"Shelby wrote a book?" She looked from me to the cover and back again. "It's so . . . bright."

"Here." I pried the paperback from her hand and ushered her to the table, where I would painstakingly steer us clear of anything resembling a serious conversation. After commenting on each element of the meal—the peppers were cut in perfect strips, the chicken was not at all dry, the potatoes were very white—my mother insisted on helping me clean up. When she entered the kitchen she stared at the counter, spellbound.

"Isn't that the crock pot you gave Shelby?"

I trod lightly. "Yes. How about some chocolate ice cream?"

"Why is it here? Are you back together?" she asked hopefully. "Is that the reason for this special dinner?"

"No, Mom. She didn't want it. She left it. That's all."

"Oh, dear. I'm sorry." Then she considered for a moment. "Who wouldn't want a crock pot?"

"Shelby, Mom. Shelby didn't want a crock pot."

Over dessert I caught my mother staring at me pityingly and in response I offered an almost manic performance to demonstrate that I was fine, just fine—happy, in fact—laughing like a maniac at her Reader's Digest jokes, springing from the couch to refill her wine glass, saying that the blind dates had not really been so bad.

"I'm so glad," she said. "Because Mrs. Sitterly's daughter Sally is lovely. She owns her own daycare center. Can you imagine?"

I could. A room full of diaper-clad, sticky-fingered puking machines.

"I think kids could cheer you up," she stated confidently as she patted my knee. "Bring you back to your old self."

I wanted to ask about this alleged old self she clearly missed, but I understood what she meant: effortlessly cheerful, consistently engaged, much more tolerant with her and even Mr. Bojangles, who I suddenly recalled had urinated on my new leather gloves with impunity last Christmas. Even Shelby, who must have paid a hundred bucks for the now piss-soaked clumps, patted the unapologetic cat on the head and *tsk*ed about aging and bladder control. Why couldn't she have been more patient with *me*?

"I'm fine," I said, though I wasn't convinced myself.

"How about another date," she said with a wink. "Get you right back in the saddle!"

When my mother left I spent the rest of the evening imagining what I would rather do than embark on another blind date: undergo a root canal, take a punch in the mouth, get thwacked with a cattle prod.

Sally Sitterly was late, but that was all right with me, the new and improved, back-in-the-saddle, determined-to-be-patient man. I tried not to think about my mother's face and how it rose and fell with the tide of events: the successive failures of her matchmaking efforts, the discovery of Shelby's book wedged under my sofa, the initial hope and subsequent disappointment triggered by her vision of the inadequate, offending crock pot. I had to hand it to her; she did not give up easily. Eight dates, each a particularly excruciating endeavor, though of course I kept the gory details to myself. These were, after all, the daughters of her friends and I was the common denominator in an equation that persistently equaled disaster. My mother just wanted me to be happy. Maybe it was my fault, this dating purgatory, for thwarting Shelby's blind date so long ago. Maybe I'd kept her from meeting the man who would have bought her the perfect gifts, supported her literary endeavors, drawn her fully into his life. The man she had not given me the chance to become. I sipped my beer. I cringed as I considered the name Sally Sitterly and the type of woman who might own a daycare center: merry, serene, hearing-impaired. *What the hell*, I thought. *Kids are all right.*

"Sorry I'm late!"

I looked up as the familiar voice registered, and there she was, all smiles and sequins, the fruit of my mother's most recent effort: Shelby.

falling forward

Faith was sipping organic aloe juice and munching Skinny Chips when she was summoned, via telephone, to spring Ed from jail for the third time that month. *What had he done now?* she wondered. The sheriff wouldn't say, but he did tell her that she had better bring $500 because this time it was bad.

She clamped down the receiver, slid her feet into the salted water churning in her footbath, and tried to put Ed out of her mind. When the phone rang again fifteen minutes later, she was elbow-deep in the chip bag sopping crumbs with her wet fingertips, her toes raking the hard plastic nubs on the floor of the Vibra-Matic.

"It'll do him good to wait," she said. "Let him think about what he's done, whatever that is."

She heard a ruckus in the background—the clanging of pots and pans, like the sound of a hubcap skittering down the road—and then Sheriff Waldon's weary voice: "Get him out of here, Faith."

By the time she arrived at the jail—really just a room with a desk and four cells—smelling of ginger-peach spray and fingering a small bump that had sprouted suddenly just above her left wrist, Ed was asleep.

"Well," said Faith to Sheriff Waldon, "I guess I'll do some shopping. I'm all out of yogurt and echinacea."

"He was cursin' up a white storm all night." The sheriff glanced over at Ed's cell. "I don't want a replay when he comes to. Please. Let's just get him up."

Faith frowned. "Well, what'd he do this time?"

Sheriff Waldon gave her a defeated look, then jerked his head derisively toward the row of cells. "Ask *him*."

Faith and Ed had been neighbors going on two years, and although they were nearly the same age—fifty-six and sixty-one, respectively—Faith felt she was a paragon of health next to Ed, a creased and rumpled man with doom etched in his face. She shook her head in sad disapproval of Ed's health regimen when she glanced over the fence to see him passed out in a lawn chair, the sun baking his pale flesh, or when she saw the cases of empty beer bottles stacked in his garage like a wall, one that sealed him off from the good things in life: early morning walks, the happy cries of grandchildren, the smell of Protose-loaf and Nuttola streaming from the oven after having been placed there by the loving hands of a health-conscious wife bent on prolonging her time with him. Ed wasn't a bad man, Faith thought, just a selfish one. She'd heard his wife had emptied the bank account and stolen off with the adorable twins, and Faith felt bad about that, no question. But didn't a part of her feel he deserved it? Couldn't she tell by the way he dropped off mowing the lawn halfway through or launched his Buick into the driveway, its fender nosed deep into the hedge after swerving home from the Tap Shoe, that he'd had it coming? Still, when Ed approached her that scalding day last month to request a favor, brushing her hand with his as it rested on the fence between them, her legs trembled slightly. Close up, he looked a little like Marvin, who'd been dead going on twenty years.

"Can you hold this for me?" he asked, passing a worn leather shaving case over the fence. Faith had once told Ed to stop by if he needed anything—*Really*, she'd said, nodding her head like a dime-store dog—and was glad he'd finally felt comfortable enough to do it, to break free, if even temporarily, of his self-imposed isolation.

She stared at the bag for a moment, thinking *drugs, jewels, the severed digits of his former wife's right hand.*

"It's money," Ed shrugged. "For when I get in trouble, which seems to be more and more these days. I appreciate it." He smiled at her, shyly, then looked away as if her gaze would wound him.

"I don't understand," said Faith. "What am I supposed to do with it?"

Ed turned to her, and she thought he looked confused, as if she'd just cracked a bad joke or asked him how to make a soya fritter.

"Right," he said, "Sheriff Waldon'll call you. I gave him your number. I appreciate it, Faith." And with that he walked off purposefully, as if late for a shareholders' meeting.

Faith took the bag inside and made a cup of tea—there was no need to rush it. She moved through the kitchen methodically, reaching for the china cup, drawing a silver spoon from the dish rack, sliding the kettle from the burner, her poker-straight spine tingling with anticipation. When she was finally perched atop the Dr. Zielbach Ergonomi-Stool, she thought about waiting to open it. Maybe tomorrow. Faith lived for moments like this: a scandalous peek into a neighbor's life. She stared at the bag, thinking. Or, more accurately, imagining. Maybe there was a love note. Or a suicide note. Who could tell with Ed? *You're pathetic* is what she finally said to herself. She then tore it open and found that Ed, who may have been a slovenly, unhealthy drunk, wasn't a liar. The case contained money, only money—$1,250.00, to be exact—and Faith was disappointed. At first she considered hiding it with her own valuables in her underwear drawer, but the thought of the rough edges of flaking leather tearing into her cotton briefs made her neck go stiff. She finally threw it onto her closet floor and refused to think about its interaction with her shoes. She would help Ed, sure. Why not? She would gain his trust; maybe she would even save him from the things he didn't know were killing him.

Marvin had been a romantic when Faith met him more than thirty years before at the Blue Goose, where she'd go for the occasional grasshopper before she discovered herbal tea and Dr. Zielbach. He'd sing Smokey Robinson songs to her, fold bar napkins into roses and insects, ignore the welts that would suddenly flame red on her face and arms when he spun her around the dance floor. No man had ever had this type of physiological effect on Faith, had excited her to the point of eruption, and she imagined each red splotch was the shape of a heart, or a wedding ring, or a part of the anatomy that would turn her face crimson. They were married three months after they met—Faith wasn't getting any younger, her mother always said—and shortly afterward Faith realized that she remained welt and hive free when Marvin licked the back of her knee or slid his fingers over her breasts. She wondered why she had been cured—she still loved him, after all—and ultimately determined that she was now content rather than happy, in love rather than in lust. But the more she eased into the comforts that a long-time relationship provided, the more Marvin wanted to recapture what Faith felt was no longer required. He wanted to take her to the Blue Goose and sing to her, though she felt silly when he reembarked on a courtship ritual that had already been successful, and she felt he was sullying the memory with this bad, albeit unwitting, parody. She just wanted to go home and read a book while Marvin watched the news.

But the more Faith wanted to be home, it seemed, the more Marvin wanted to be out playing her Romeo, caressing her hand while crooning oldies at the piano bar or dipping her as they waltzed at Sparle's. In public the welts and hives resurfaced, and that's when Faith understood that they had not been the physiological effects of love but something much more sinister: an outer manifestation of her inner discomfort; she was not bursting from love but from embarrassment. She suddenly recalled not the rich baritone of Marvin's young voice as he belted out a soulful version of "My Girl" or the strength of his arm as he held her parallel to the dance floor, but the disapproving stares, the forced smiles, the comments that in retrospect were not as friendly as they had once sounded.

She'd meant to tell Marvin, gently, that she no longer enjoyed his overtures, his overblown displays of affection, but he preempted her. After twelve years and seven months of marriage, twelve years and seven months of wining and dancing and dipping, twelve years and seven months of welts and hives and public inflammations, he fell into a plate of linguini at Marco's and didn't get up. Faith blamed herself for the heart attack: she should have watched his drinking, cooked less meat, convinced him to exercise. The day after Marvin's funeral Faith dragged the industrial trash bin from the garage to the middle of the kitchen floor and chucked into it every bit of food in the house: canned peaches in syrup, frozen T-bones, orange soda, garlic bologna, hamburger buns, even butter. For three days she drank water and ate nothing, unplugged the phone and let the doorbell ring. Then, after she could no longer tolerate her hunger headache, she searched the directory for a health food store and slowly traded her grief for carrot fritters and vegan tacos, Tai Chi and yoga.

She'd forgotten about the hives and rashes until Ed entered her life. They had returned with a vengeance when the neighbors stared over fences to watch her offer Ed a bag of homemade granola or to share the health-food-store circular with him, or even when she climbed into her car to drive to the jail, Ed's money in hand, as if they knew she was going to fetch the man she thought looked like her former husband, one she might save in place of the one she couldn't.

Faith had dipped into Ed's bag twice before, both times after Ed had been dragged in for drunk and disorderly after putting up a stink at the Tap Shoe. This time the sheriff told her to bring twice as much bail money, and she figured as she entered the jail that Ed had moved from being a pain in the ass to full-scale criminality.

"Ed," she called through the thick iron bars on his cell, but Ed remained a snoring, undulating heap. Faith turned to the sheriff.

"Does he have a car to drive?" she asked, having just then understood that it may have been impounded.

"Yep," said the sheriff, smirking.

"Is he fit to drive?" she asked, and Waldon nodded as he counted out the money, plunking each bill onto his desk.

"Well, then," said Faith, "let him." She turned to leave, and Sheriff Waldon *tsk*ed.

"What?" said Faith. "*What*?"

"He's a lucky man, Faith. Not many women would put up with him . . . with *this*." He glanced around the small jail and his eyes landed on Ed.

Faith was appalled. "I don't *put up* with him," she said, caressing the rash that had suddenly spread across her right shoulder. "He's my neighbor, that's all. I'm just being neighborly."

"Well, sure," said Sheriff Waldon. "That's all I'm saying."

"Who else has he got?" Faith said defensively, knowing those words would make Waldon think she pitied Ed. But how else could she justify her behavior? How else could she explain her trips to the jail, cash in hand, to bail him out for the third time that month? She could say she was a lonely, pathetic widow with nothing else to do, or she could convince him that she was engaged in a humanitarian effort of the highest sort, or she could say that she was fond of Ed, that the fact that he *took* the circulars and seemed to at least consider the value of tofu bites had awakened something in her. But all of these things were too close to the truth to admit, even to herself. *Damn Ed*, she thought as she exited the jail. *Damn him to hell.*

Faith was in her living room in mountain pose an hour later when she heard Ed's Buick clanging up the street. She was fully prepared to give him the ultimatum: help yourself or I can't help you. The night before she'd dreamed about Marvin, who turned into Ed and then back into Marvin so gradually that one man's head topped the other's body. She would tell him this, all of it, make him see it her way. She exited her house at a good clip, but when Ed pulled into the driveway she noticed it: he had been in an accident. A strange one. The driver's side door was caved in, the left front quarter panel was missing, and the antenna was bent double. Still, she stalked across the mowed section of Ed's lawn toward his driveway with resolve, sensing eyes peering at her from behind curtains and hedges, lawn mowers and garages. As Ed struggled toward the passenger door, muttering and cursing all the way, Faith rubbed the dry patch of skin on her left elbow that had suddenly burst into a flaming itch. The curses rose several octaves when Ed couldn't force open the door, and when he started kicking at it Faith rushed to his aid.

"Keep your shirt on," she snapped, and when she looked at Ed through the cracked passenger window she saw a little boy; his clothes were rumpled, his hair a mess and—the most shocking of all—he was crying. She opened the door quite easily and noticed then that the inside handle was missing. Ed stared at the dashboard, breathing heavily, but made no effort to get out of the car. He looked defeated, worn down, resigned to spending the rest of his life perched uncomfortably on the cracked vinyl seat. A few of the neighborhood kids gathered at the foot of the driveway, mouths agape and fingers pointing, and Mrs. Bushnell across the street was on tiptoe, leaning against her broom to get a better view of the mangled carcass of Ed's car.

"Ed," said Faith quietly, "let's get you inside."

Ed turned to her then, his eyes red and swollen, and sighed. "I can't," he said.

"Sure, you can," said Faith, and in one motion her inflamed elbow was hooked under Ed's bulk and pulling as if her life depended on it. Ed tapped his feet on the passenger-side mat, as if checking to see if they still worked, and slid them slowly toward the door. After rocking to-and-fro several times, he exited the car on shaky legs and the neighborhood kids started cheering.

Once inside, Faith deposited Ed's mass on the sofa and then, to avoid giving the neighbors an encore, ran to her house via the back door to retrieve two Edamame Rice Bowls, some mango juice and her arnica gel (surely Ed's muscles were stiff from sleeping on that rack Sheriff Waldon called a bed). But when she returned to Ed's place she heard the distant buzz of a beehive, a motorboat: he was snoring into a paisley sofa cushion. Just then it started to rain, and as Faith placed the tube of gel on the coffee table beside Ed she felt eyes boring tiny holes into the small of her back. Turning suddenly, her throat seizing up, she saw it there, not six feet away, its scaly feet and long, threadlike-fingers splayed against the aquarium wall. As Faith approached with trepidation, the tiny creature remained still but for its eyes, which followed her as she inspected its scaly green body, its long, narrow tail, the fringe on its oversized head. "Why, you're a lizard," she said. "And you must be a hungry one."

The cupboard beneath the aquarium was empty, so Faith heated one of the rice bowls in Ed's microwave before searching his cavernous cupboards for a small container. All she found were two cans of Campbell's Chunky soup, some Hamburger Helper and a bag of cheese popcorn. *Processed food*, she thought, *would drive anyone to drink*; she had to stop herself from trashing it all.

"Here you go, darlin'," she said as she flipped open the aquarium lid and scooped three teaspoonfuls of rice into the creature's corroded dish. But it remained immobile, its stony silhouette reflected in the wall of glass adjacent to it, evidently imbued with the patience and fortitude of its prehistoric ancestors.

Faith swayed slowly from side to side and watched the lizard's eyes rotate to keep its gaze fixed on her.

"Why, you're a little hypnotist," she said. "You're really something."

She smiled at the little green dinosaur because she believed it liked her. As a child she felt she had the ability to communicate with animals, driving the baboons into a frenzy at the zoo by planting thoughts of freedom and rebellion into their heads, or calming a skittish horse by speaking gently into its ear of brown oats and alfalfa. She never told anyone about it—after all, who would believe her? But she felt a connection to the little green reptile, and so she told it to march right up to its food dish and eat. It must have liked her quite a lot, she thought, because it remained propped against the glass, its tiny fingers twitching, saliva dripping from its puckered mouth.

Faith didn't know how long she and the creature stared at one another, silently commiserating about the challenging task of befriending Ed. At one point she thought she saw the little green head nod, its black eyes full of the wisdom of the ages, and although at the time she did not know it, somewhere inside the recesses of her heart she began to nurture an admiration for the wreck of a man who lay snoring on the sofa behind her, a man with the wisdom or intuition or simple dumb luck to acquire such a stoic and majestic pet.

"My wife never liked him." Faith turned to see Ed rising slowly, almost gracefully, into an upright position. He rubbed his head and nodded toward the aquarium. "Little Richard," he said. "Carmen never liked him."

"Why not?"

Ed took a deep breath. "Well, first off, he stinks. And he drools. And he never liked *her*."

"He's just following his nature," she said.

"That's right," said Ed. "That's right. Come to think of it, that was something my wife didn't like about me either."

"Well," said Faith, choosing her words carefully, "who we are is who we are. But how we behave . . . well, now *that* we can control." She looked to Little Richard, her confidante, her sounding board.

Ed just laughed. "I wouldn't place any money on *that*," he said. "Take last night, for instance."

Faith was wildly curious about the events that had culminated in

Ed's bail being doubled and his car looking like it had lost the demolition derby. But she held back; she would emulate Little Richard's detached calm.

"It was Carmen," he said. "My ex. I don't hate her, although I'd like to. She lives in Oakley with some guy owns a junkyard. I'll tell you what, that guy can take a car apart." Ed laughed, rubbed his left eye. Then he stared right through Faith, and she knew he was watching Carmen with someone else, watching his car being broken apart like a puzzle.

"Ed," she said, "you don't have to talk about it."

"She come sashaying into the Tap Shoe like she owned the place," he said, "wearing some checked ruffled number looked like a goddamn kitchen curtain—pardon my French—hanging onto her grease monkey like he was a magnet. I ignored them, I did." He looked at Faith, his expression one of defiant sincerity.

"Why, sure you did," said Faith. "What else were you supposed to do?"

"Then the little monkey says, 'That him? That the guy? You there,' and Carmen's trying to shush him but he keeps on until I offer to buy them a drink. How do you like that?"

"That was very generous," said Faith.

"The monkey walks over and calls me Diamond Jim. 'Diamond Jim', he says, 'big shot. Buying rounds with money you stole from this lady and her twin boys.' He points to Carmen, and she looks sorry. Sorry that she lied about the money, sorry she came into the Tap Shoe in the first place, sorry she's tangled up with this monkey. She tells him let's go but he keeps on until his voice becomes like kindling, like a lit fuse, like a trigger. I get up to leave—Boyle's already reaching for the phone—but then I'm suddenly outside myself. It's like I'm watching someone else punch this guy in the gut, lay him out like a rug."

Faith, simultaneously exhilarated and repulsed, couldn't speak.

"Maybe if he'd gotten in a punch they'd have hauled him in too. Instead, they scraped him up and threw some ice on his face. Boyle didn't notice it until he locked up, but he came straight to the jail to tell me the monkey'd taken a crowbar to my car—had the crowbar and everything. Found it hooked into the passenger-side window."

"Well, that's cowardly," said Faith. "Downright cowardly." She felt the unfairness of it. She felt sorry for the defenseless Buick, its cracked windshield, a gaping hole where the grille once was. As if to express his outrage, Little Richard began leaping about the aquarium, his wiry fingers hooking into the mesh on the ceiling.

"He wants out," said Ed. "I don't blame him. It's no good to be locked up. People pointing fingers, staring." Ed watched his reflection in the aquarium glass. "It's no good," he said, shaking his head slowly. "I should let him out."

"Let him out! What if he gets into something? He could get hurt."

"I don't mean let him out here," he said. "I mean let him go."

"You mean set him *free*?" Faith stared at Little Richard as he dangled from the mesh, watched his small chest bounce with each quick breath, tried to read his thoughts. "Yes," she finally said, "I think it's what he wants."

"It's what we all want."

"Where would you take him?"

"I dunno. How 'bout a swamp? Somewhere there's plenty of bugs."

Faith wrung her hands; she hadn't expected this. Just like Marvin, Ed had preempted her, stolen the moment she had selected to make her point by embroiling her in another quandary, though she soon realized that this one did not feel fraught or even overly complicated.

"So now he can change his life," she said. "Just like that."

"Yes," Ed said, the words hovering over them like a benediction. "Just like that."

Ed took a deep breath as if readying himself for a long stint underwater, then rose and without a word approached the aquarium, opened the lid and scooped Little Richard into his palm. "Okay, buddy," he said, turning to Faith. "Let's go." She wasn't sure if he was talking to her or to Little Richard, but then Ed took her hand and the three exited Ed's house to the amusement and great satisfaction of the neighbors.

They marched down the front steps and climbed into the passenger side of the Buick after the door opened with an excruciating whine. Faith would have offered to drive, but she'd grown so flustered when Ed took her hand that she'd simply followed. Slowly and silently they made their way toward the outskirts of town. The driver's side mirror flew off like a projectile when Ed made a right-hand turn at Brimley, and as they bumped along the gravel road that led to the Racine Nature Preserve, the license plate skittered off into the gutter.

"It's no good being locked up," Ed said to Little Richard as they sat on the damp earth near the edge of a small pond. "Eating whatever they give you, being stared at or ignored. Being called a freak."

"No one called you a freak," said Faith, and Ed turned to her.

"I meant him." He nodded at Little Richard. "Carmen said he was a freak of nature. Some sort of genetic mix-up. When I told her that Little Richard's heart was bigger than hers, she broke all our dishes."

As she watched Little Richard, his eyes fixed on Ed, his left front foot tapping Ed's wristwatch, Faith was convinced he understood, and she was suddenly happy he would be forever freed from his fishbowl, his glass house, his observation tank. She thought of her neighbors then, how she'd allowed their stares to penetrate her skin, how she had put herself on display, made herself vulnerable by obsessing over what others thought.

Faith placed her hand on Ed's, and Little Richard stepped onto it slowly and carefully, his head jerking to the sunset tunes of crickets and bullfrogs, dragonflies and peepers. "Are you happy?" she asked Little Richard. Just then he flicked his tail and opened his mouth wide, revealing a small red tongue, little serrated teeth, a razor-sharp smile.

The sun hung low in the sky, casting small shadows across the water and the stunted trees that fringed the pond.

"Well," said Ed as he leaned toward Little Richard and stroked his chin, "I guess this is *arrivederci*. Happy trails, big fella." He sniffed, rubbed his nose with a balled fist.

"We don't have to do this," said Faith.

"Yes," said Ed. "It's the *only* thing to do."

Little Richard jolted upright in Faith's palm, and she imagined she felt his heart beat as she spoke to him silently of fresh grass, of murky water, of freedom in all its pain and possibility. *This is your chance*, she thought. *Here is a fresh start.* For a while Little Richard stayed, rigid and immobile, his feet hooked in, rooted to his past like a myth. But when the moon took the sky and the sun bowed in homage to a new day, he sprung skyward, over the embankment and toward the water, falling forward into a new life.

turn of the wind

Ben was sixty-four, stubborn. Unprepared. He'd been tired, disoriented, and irritable for months, although the latter symptom was nothing unusual. When he finally visited Dr. Ludrow, the man promptly ignored his request to go easy on the tests, ordering a spinal tap to see if it was meningitis, an MRI to check for tumors or strokes, and psychological and cognitive tests to uncover depression. "And if it's none of those," he said without batting an eye, "then it's probably dementia." Three weeks later Ben sat opposite Dr. Ludrow in his oak-planked office holding a form that summarized the test results, one that diagnosed a high probability of Alzheimer's. Ben made a copy and gave it to the research supervisor at the lab where he had explored the complex nature of solid matter for the past forty years.

"I'm not giving two weeks' notice," he said. "I hope you understand."

"But, Ben," she said, "your project is just taking off. We can accommodate your treatments, your schedule, whatever."

"I don't think I can—"

"Of course you can," she said. "Take a few days off. Relax. We'll talk about this next week."

Phone against her ear, she marched from the lab as if it had all been settled. Ben wondered if she believed that relaxation was a remedy, that a few days off would cure Alzheimer's, but he knew better. His work drew funding like a magnet, and while he'd always known that this is all that mattered, his supervisor's blatant admission infuriated him. He stalked to the storage room, yanking a cardboard box from a high metal shelf before emptying file cabinets and loading crystal specimens inside. His arm, as if by its own volition, swept across his desk and sent pens and framed photographs flying. The lab techs looked up from folders and computer screens at the sound of shattering glass, but none dared approach.

As he drove home, the large box propped on the passenger seat beside him, Ben understood that no one had his experience or expertise and that they would struggle to continue his projects. The techs had watched him countless times as he tested unconventional crystal hosts in large glass cases, but it was the times they couldn't watch—when he rushed to the lab at night or during weekends—that made him certain they could not continue his work. But he didn't care. Why should a young upstart take credit for his innovations while he sat, glassy-eyed and drooling, unable to comprehend his former genius?

Ben had begun his ground-breaking research two years earlier by testing environments that favor crystal growth—first water, then sediment, and finally gel mixtures—and found that the crystals prospered in outlandish materials. He grew calcite crystals in peaches, lead iodide in grape jelly. He found that growing crystals in gel is disarmingly simple, inexpensive, and effective as gels allow crystals to grow while offering enough resistance to keep them from mutating out of control. Crystals grown slowly and thoughtfully, he learned, were almost always more perfect than those grown in haste. His method had opened new avenues for research on many substances that had never been grown in single-cell form, fostering the discovery of how to make drugs found only in plants and microbes synthetically by learning the drug's growth pattern which, like all solid matter, begins with a solitary cell. Things were, as his supervisor so eloquently stated, *taking off*.

It was painful to leave behind the hope of discovery, but what more subtly nagged him was that he couldn't allow anyone else that hope. Being selfish and proprietary are traits not uncommon in scientists, but

Ben knew that he was acting like the angry child in possession of the only ball on the playground. It was *his*, after all.

For weeks he stared at the cardboard box, convinced that tucked into the crystals' translucent folds and angled pleats were answers to age-old medical questions and refutations to long-held theories that could be extracted only by someone fully connected to his intellectual and emotional faculties. But if that someone couldn't be him, it would be no one. He hid the box in the barn and tried not to think about it.

Ben had always loved working with his hands, playing with Tinker Toys as a child, building models with his father, constructing crystal replicas for investors from Sony and directors of the American Medical Association. Dr. Ludrow recommended that he take up some sort of craft, claiming that the concentration required in the physical act of creation would relieve his stress by focusing his attention on something other than his deteriorating brain.

"So I can slip into mental oblivion unawares?" he asked.

"Something like that," the doctor said absently.

He was a busy man, but Ben resented being dismissed while still in possession of his rational mind. "Young man," he said, "let me tell you something: I am a research scientist. I have contributed to the perfection of the instruments you shove down peoples' throats and up their asses in the name of medicine."

"I'm sorry," he said. "I didn't mean to—"

"You didn't mean to what? Tell a man who has explored the geometry of order for forty years that his brain is scrambled, that his career is over, that the only certainty in his future is bedlam?"

But that very afternoon Ben decided there would be no harm in making weathervanes as therapy. After all, how precise do you have to be with functional art that sits far beyond the scrutiny of the naked eye?

Years ago, when he lived on a small farm in upstate New York, his father, an artist and a member of both the Preservation Society of Newport and the New York State Historic Trust, was commissioned to make a detailed weathercock that now sits atop the Museum of American Folk Art in New York City. Ben recalled rolling the glass eyes of the five-foot, one-hundred-seventy-two-pound legless rooster in his hand, admiring not so much the size and shape but the luster of the globes, the way the sun refracted through them to create rainbows on the barn floor. He even thought about stealing one, telling his father that he had lost it, but had been inducted into the project and had, somewhere along the way, developed a greater loyalty to the rooster than to his penchant for shiny objects. He was not sure if the sudden desire to again make weathervanes was induced by nostalgia or by a misfired synapse.

Though he'd lived in Pittsfield most of his adult life, Ben seldom visited the town proper as he was always at the lab, either physically or mentally. But bored by sudden retirement and in need of craft supplies, he began to frequent the tiny center of commerce, shyly contemplating the people who entered the beauty salon, the hardware store, the quaint shops, waving hello to his new neighbors—Braelynn and Jake and their three children whose names he could never recall. He started eating at the local diner and was sorry he didn't lie when asked by Esther, a veteran waitress who persistently delivered meals to the wrong tables, what he did for fun.

"You don't say! Listen to this, Opal," she yelled to one of her pink-aproned cohorts and pointed at Ben. "He makes weathervanes. You know, them things on the roof."

Opal, coffee pot dangling from her right hand, pivoted toward his table, either keenly interested or keenly polite, he thought. "What kind of weathervanes do you make?" she asked, her blue eyes twinkling. At least he thought—or hoped—they were twinkling.

Before he could respond, Esther broke in. "Weathervanes have roosters on 'em."

"Well," he said, "I don't make roosters."

"Right," she said as if catching on to the obvious after her initial mistake. "Chickens."

"No, I make weathervanes with mythological figures," he said. "You know, Circe, Zeus, Apollo."

"Oh, like Cleopatra," Esther said proudly.

"Cleopatra was not a mythological figure," he said.

"You mean she was real?"

"Yes."

"I'll be damned."

So this is it, he thought. *This is where I am: alone, in Pittsfield, losing my faculties among people who think that Pluto is nothing more than a cartoon character.*

And this is when Opal touched his shoulder so lightly he thought he'd imagined it, looked at him for a brief eternity during which he knew they were conspirators against the ignorance and foolishness in the world, or at least the ignorance and foolishness in the Pittsfield diner. As she refilled his coffee cup he wondered which weathervane figure Opal might like: Io, the beautiful mortal princess of Argos, or Minerva, the goddess of wisdom, or the valiant Diomede who fought at Troy.

Later that week when he met Mrs. Winston at the diner to discuss the specifics of her weathervane, he was immediately exposed to the trials of human indecision, something he seldom encountered in the lab.

"It's a surprise for my husband," she said. "What do *you* think we should have?"

They stared at each other for several seconds. He did not tell her that she was his first client, or that he had lost all confidence in his ability to deliver what his newspaper ad had promised: to mold any mythological figure the customer desired.

"What type of building is it for?" he asked.

"Oh," she said. "What a good question! It's for the granary. We grow corn. Our old one blew off last year. My husband jokes that the rooster just up and flew away." She laughed, her delicate fist over her mouth, and that's when it occurred to him.

"How about Ceres?" he asked. "The goddess of the harvest."

"What does she look like?"

An odd question, he thought, since even the most detailed weathervane appears only in silhouette. "She'll have windblown hair and an armload of cornstalks. I'll make sure you can see those."

When Esther delivered the next table's ham and eggs to them, Ben asked for an extra napkin and drew on it what he promised would be a one-of-a-kind model. Mrs. Winston gave him a check on the spot.

The weathervane, made from local sheet iron, towered majestically over the Winstons' cornfields, and soon orders trickled in from all over the county. Orpheus now cradles a lyre atop the music school, Neptune rides wrought iron waves on the fishery, and Mercury, whose winged feet had to be recast several times, sits on a cupola above the *Pittsfield Gazette*. Ben was interviewed for a story the paper ran the day the vane was mounted, and in it there is a quote that he does not recall giving: "Knowledge of the past provides a sense of the continuity of the human struggle. Our heritage lies in legends, tales and myths." He liked the quote but for the final line: "My weathervane is a story on a stick."

Of course he never stopped thinking about his crystals, foolishly tucked under a workbench in the barn as if the "Out of sight, out of mind" adage could bear on his long-term connection to them. Sometimes he even thought about his ex-wife, for she was inextricably bound to the crystals, the images pairing themselves through a convoluted process he had never been able to chart. The memories came through sounds, mostly, the images more real to him than their wedding photo, which still hung on the living room wall. She didn't want it, and he never bothered to take it down. When he opened the barn door, he recalled the wooden planks creaking under his weight as he knelt on Millicent's front porch and placed the ring, still in the unopened box, into her outstretched hand.

"Yes," she said, although he had not yet said anything.

They did not proceed slowly and thoughtfully. They were married within a month. They were twenty-four years old. They moved from New York to Massachusetts so Ben could accept a tenure-track teaching position at MIT, and he listened to those wooden planks groan once more when they said goodbye to Millie's parents.

He taught for only two years before becoming so engrossed in research that he lectured only occasionally and instead grew crystals from floor to ceiling in a dedicated lab. Millie always complained that he worked too much, but she never griped about the emerald earrings or the ruby pin. Once, though, when he gave her an albite bracelet as an anniversary gift, she'd acted as if he'd proffered a severed finger. "What's this *made* of?" she asked sheepishly, but he was already aware of her ability to discriminate between the expensive and the merely beautiful. "It's a moonstone," he said, "powerful for bringing good fortune in love." To his knowledge, she has never worn the bracelet.

Unlike crystals, weathervanes, once "grown," were dead to Ben. Charming, certainly, but simple, empty, inert. They were not revealing or resplendent like crystals, the flowers of the mineral kingdom. Scintillating colors in rocks, reflections from polished faces of cut glass, the brilliance of diamonds are all gifts bestowed by crystals, which are precisely ordered walls of atoms, like translucent panels in a funhouse that are erected at fixed angles to amuse and delight us. Even though the internal structure of a crystal is a testament to orderly repetition, every crystal maintains a slight error in its pattern, a naturally occurring and unavoidable flaw, like a mole on the cheek of a beautiful woman. This knowledge was his permission to strive for perfection in crystallography, knowing he could extract perfect solutions from imperfect models. Weathervanes, however, offered beauty without the hope of anything more: cures, answers, discoveries. *What can I do*, he wondered as he sat on the lumpy bench at the diner sipping from a cup of cold coffee, *to make the construction of a weathervane akin to the growth of a crystal, to make the work more meaningful?* His mind was held hostage until Opal approached him and broke that dark, dark spell. Opal, he thought, is lovely; she radiates like a blue star sapphire, and when he's in the diner he can hardly look away. Opal pulled him from those circular thoughts, the wind tunnel of his mind, the roar of the void.

"Opal," he said as she set his toast and a pot of coffee onto the table before him, "let me tell you something: The external shape of any crystal is merely a manifestation of the arrangement of the component atoms."

"Excuse me?"

"I think you must be very beautiful inside," he said. When she blushed and dropped into an awkward curtsy, he fell in love.

A widow who'd taken the waitressing job because she was lonely, Opal didn't grow glassy-eyed like Millie often had when Ben spoke; on the contrary, she had a genuine interest in the building blocks of this planet. Sometimes when she wasn't too busy they'd spill salt onto the table and inspect the simple cube-shaped crystals with a magnifying lens, or they'd study the angles of cleavage planes in ice cubes. He'd given Opal a small microscope after she'd expressed an interest in crystallography, and it wasn't unusual to see her propped against the counter, her eye fixed to the metal shaft.

"Look at this!" she'd shout, and her excitement was customary for someone newly introduced to the micro-architecture of the world. Baking soda, concrete, aspirin—Opal was interested in everything.

For days he mulled over whether he should ask Opal out for coffee, what he'd do if she declined. Lately, when he concentrated his senses grew sharp—the buzz of a circling mosquito sounded like a bandsaw, the fibers in lettuce felt like thick ropes, the wedge-shaped corners in sugar crystals stabbed his tongue when he sipped coffee. It was horribly distracting and made him uncertain about everything until the morning Opal set down a glass of water and said, "You know that 'crystal' is Greek for 'clear ice'?" He took this as a sign and asked her *something*, though he'll be damned if he can recall what it was.

Opal was nothing like Ben's ex-wife, who only pretended to be interested in his work. Millie would say things like "Pass the sodium chloride" or "Don't take me for granite," and he found it difficult to laugh at comments like those more than once. He often worked long hours, and sometimes when he crawled into bed in the middle of the night and ran his fingers along the silken folds of her Givenchy nightdress, she'd say, "Go to halite."

In time, Millie picked up on more sophisticated lab terminology. She'd stare into an ice cream container and say, "There is an unwelcome manifestation of crystallization in here," or she'd squint at a moldy round of Brie and say, "This cheese is saturated with tartrate."

"That's my girl," he'd say.

It was no longer cute, however, when he, doubled over in pain from chronic gallstones, heard her talking on the phone to her sister Chloe.

"He has calcium carbonate deposits in his organs," she said. "They've grown up to five millimeters in six weeks. His gallbladder is quite the crystal conductor."

Millie's vocabulary may have grown, but her patience with his schedule and his devotion to the study of crystals remained small, strained, stunted. Maybe that was *their* point of communion–impatience–for Ben was in a perpetual rush to discover or to be discovered. In his ardor for results he botched experiments, alienated colleagues, and angered supervisors, even after he had become a minor celebrity in crystallography circles. Millie always sided with the offended party.

"You take your job too seriously," she said.

"I am altering the course of civilization."

"Walt Disney altered the course of civilization," she said, "and he didn't take himself so seriously."

Last week, as he watched a geology documentary on public television, Ben flew into a rage, pitching a china bowl into the living room wall and flattening his claw foot coffee table. *Has a filmmaker ever credited a crystallographer with* anything? he wondered. *Did they know that it was not geologists or physicists but crystallographers who uncovered the mystery of how a glacier can flow over mountains without splitting apart, why a hair stretches before breaking, why just one ounce of gold can be hammered thin enough to cover a football field or rolled into a wire thirty miles long?* He took his pills—two blue and a small green—and shut off the television, then sat back down on the sofa and stared at the wall to avoid looking at the debris scattered about the floor, Millie hijacking his thoughts once more. She had insisted he help choose wallpaper for the restored farmhouse in which he now stewed, and he recalled how he had stood, awestruck, in the home décor showroom as she pored over three-ring binders containing custom samples.

"We have no imagination," he said.

Millie, who was honing what would be an exemplary ability to ignore him, hummed as she flipped the pages.

"Can I help you, sir?" asked a young salesman with baggy pants and tufts of red hair that jutted from his scalp like a fountain.

"All of this wallpaper contains precisely repetitive designs."

"Yes."

"Why is that?"

The boy seemed confused. "That's what people want."

"Exactly," Ben said. "Man is a three-dimensional creature who surrounds himself with two-dimensional objects adorned with repetitive motifs. Did you know that the pattern of a crystal does not differ from the pattern of a carpet in any significant way? The two patterns are distinguished *only* by the additional dimension in the crystal."

"I'll get the manager," he said.

When Ben tried to special-order three doublewide rolls of wallpaper with a minor flaw in the flower pattern, the manager pointed and said, "The defective rolls are in back."

They did not buy wallpaper that day, and Millie accused him of embarrassing her as they drove home.

"Why can't you have normal conversations with people?" she said.

"I had a legitimate question."

"Why can't you leave your work in the lab?"

"My work isn't confined to a lab," he said. "Look at this." He tapped the car's radio display, held up his wristwatch, touched Millie's earring. "These are products of crystal formation," he said. "Should *they* be confined to a lab?"

Millie stared blankly through the window. "Stop," she said. "Just stop talking for ten minutes so I can pretend you and your crystals don't exist."

"Then who's driving?" he laughed. "Can you go without music—"

"Stop," she said, and he did.

In time Millie became a darting electron, bouncing from one affair to the next during the final phase of their marriage. Ben, of course, was too busy sketching calcite rhombohedra or splitting mica flakes to stop her from driving her boyfriend's Volvo to her attorney's office to file for divorce. In her defense, she called to say that she was sorry (not about the divorce, but about the fact that he had driven her to it). They volleyed accusations via telephone, and in an accelerated argument covered ground it takes most couples a lifetime to travel.

"I've got to go, Ben," she finally said. "The papers will arrive in the mail. Please don't hate me."

"What the halite," he said and hung up.

Ben continued to sit on the sofa until his breaths came evenly. Then he rose and made his way to the barn by starlight, working hard to stay rooted to the present when the door creaked open. There it was: his box of crystals, one side ablaze in a moonbeam refracted through the barn's uppermost window. He reached under the workbench, slid his hands along the dusty cardboard, worked his fingers around the sharp edges. Then he sat on the floor and opened the box before holding each crystal to the light, allowing the moon to set their facets blinking across the walls like a thousand untold thoughts, a flurry of withheld secrets, a distant constellation of hope. He imagined his brain as a funhouse, an erratic maze of crystalized walls, brilliant but flawed, and this frightened him until his mind spun like a roulette wheel and he let his thought fall into the slot chance selected. It did not land on a memory of his supervisor or his colleagues at the lab, or even Millie or the dumbstruck salesclerk at the wallpaper store but, to his sudden shock, on Opal. Was Opal still working at the diner? Was he meeting her there this weekend for coffee cake and antique-store browsing afterward? Had this already happened yesterday, or perhaps ages before? He thought about Opal, compelling her into his current reality as he sat on the floor, crystals clutched to his chest, staring through the window at the darkening night. Slowly he recalled her soft white hair, the pink apron cinched around her tiny waist, her suggestion that they check Bahle's for some moonstone earrings the coming Saturday after her shift. As the stars crawled across the sky, he remembered watching a meteor shower with Opal, though when that was he could not say. He had promised to teach her the names of the constellations as she pointed her slender finger up at the cosmos. But now, as he gazed through the window trying to locate Pleiades, Cassiopeia, Orion, they fell together and broke apart as if in a shaken beaker. So he renamed them: The Dominoes, whose movements affect every other cluster in the solar system; The Biased Tunnel, which draws in and skews all cosmic matter; Benjamin, a prophet penning the secret stories of the stars; and Opal, the endless knot, the triangle of balance, insight, and tranquility.

WHEN THE COUNTY COMMISSIONER REQUESTED a weathervane for the courthouse and asked if he could do something with scales, Ben was thrown into confusion.

"I think we've veered into astrology," he said gently.

"Ah."

They stared at each other. "But I can do scales," he said, momentarily relishing the easy symmetry of a project, one that would be child's play compared to some of the complex mechanisms he'd assembled over the past several months.

"What was on top of the Parthenon?" the man asked, and Ben chuckled at the unwitting parallel he'd drawn between the meeting quarters of a great civilization and the judicial center of a town where pigs had the right of way.

"There is a triton atop the Tower of the Winds that still stands in Athens," he said. "I could make that."

"All right," he answered in a way that made Ben certain the man had no idea what to expect.

The vane was mounted on Founder's Day, and Ben, along with a cast that included practically every resident of Pittsfield, was asked to give a short speech on a makeshift stage near the courthouse lawn. He told the crowd that the Greeks had invented the weathervane as part of their investigation into natural phenomena because to them the winds had personalities and vanes were oracles portending a fruitful harvest or a deadly famine. He then, more and more the savvy businessman, spoke of vanes nostalgically.

"Weathervanes, like friends, always tell the truth," he said. "We may not like the turn of the wind, but the weathervane foretells the future in no uncertain terms."

He spoke for a while before he noticed the confused, almost stricken, faces in the crowd.

"Under appropriate circumstances, a crystal may extend its boundaries and grow," he said. "Unlike living things, a crystal grows by the addition of atoms to its external surface. When this does not take place too rapidly, the new material is added in layers along rational lattice planes."

Then someone was tapping his shoulder, and he was escorted off the stage by a gentle hand on his elbow.

The following afternoon when Esther brought him a bowl of lime Jell-O he didn't order just before announcing her retirement, he was thrown into a quandary. He could not eat lime Jell-O. He could not eat any Jell-O, for that matter, for he saw crystals writhing in the muck, fighting the Jell-O for space, engaging in a savage expansion war.

"Esther—"

"I'm moving to Jersey to help my daughter with her new baby," she interrupted. "He's thirty-four pounds if he's an ounce, and he's only three months old. The doctor said Dwayne's the fattest baby he ever saw. Said he's gonna be in kid's clothes before he can even crawl. Said he's a mutant baby. He was on the news and everything."

"That's wonderful," Ben said.

"I got a good back," she said thoughtfully.

"About this Jell-O. I'm afraid I can't eat it."

"Why not?"

"Esther," he said. "I didn't order this."

"Sure you did," she said before trotting off to poke a photo of her new grandchild into another customer's face.

Opal came to him then. "Here you go," she said, winking as she slid a white plate with wheat toast and a pot of black coffee onto the table.

The shower awakened him, and he was startled to see a pair of white support hose dangling from the bedpost. This wasn't a dream; he made sure of that by tugging his hair, licking his lips, running pink apron strings through his fingers. Opal emerged from the bathroom, and when she saw his distress, she patiently recounted their night together—lobster bisque at The Cove, coffee and tiramisu at Annie's, a glass of red wine and a cozy fire in his living room—animating the events, pulling them from the abyss into a reality he could live, or relive: the chunky bisque delivered by a young woman who said she was studying forensics in college, the coffee too hot to drink until after the dessert was long finished, the corkscrew Opal had gently removed from his hand as he struggled to thread it into the stopper of a Petite Sirah he had been saving for thirty years. Oh, how he happily recalled that together they sought the flavors of blackberry, pepper, plum and licorice on their tongues, how the combined taste persisted until he fell asleep with Opal's warmth pressed against him. She was his memory, his cryptographer, his guide; he would mold for her a weathervane in the form of Ariadne, whose ball of red thread led her lover out of the Minotaur's labyrinth. He recalled without prompting the reason they had celebrated, had poured the burgundy wine into crystal flutes and toasted Ben's career, his contribution to science and medicine, his wish—while the generous impulse bloomed in him—to augment that contribution.

After breakfast he held Opal's hand and led her to the barn. They opened the box, and he removed the citrine crystals, the bismuth, the aventurine. When he stared at them he did not see answers and refutations, solutions and equations, angles and planes. He saw something that was, simply, beautiful. He couldn't perform a simple cleavage calculation, so instead he held them up to Opal and said, "Look." He stated the obvious: "Citrine is lemon-colored, bismuth is blue, and aventurine is speckled with glistening scales of mica. This, as I recall, is important."

Opal lined the bottom of the box with his notes, nine thick, college-ruled books cramped with calculations, formulas, hypotheses. Together they wrapped the geodes, the agates, the crystals in tissue paper before placing them carefully onto the tablets, then poured in Styrofoam pellets before resealing the box with reinforced tape. They addressed it to Ben's former supervisor at the lab, and Opal promised to mail it the following morning.

They spent the rest of the day at the park observing sand crystals, and that evening they lay in bed, her back pressed to his ribs. He watched Opal's tourmaline earrings glinting in a moonbeam on the window ledge where she'd purposely left them, a flawed yet perfect gift.

honesty above all else

I've never told anyone this story, and I'm only telling you now because Mrs. O'Leary is dead. You don't need to know my name—what's it matter? I grew up in Corktown in Detroit, live in the same Carpenter Gothic on Church that my great-grandparents lived in. Against all odds, Corktown has survived—bravery, gentrification, the luck of the Irish? But back in '99 when it happened, everything was going to hell. You couldn't count on things anymore the way the Carmodys and the McNallys could count on trains to plow into Michigan Grand Central to the south and scatter tourists onto the doorsteps of Limerick's Pub and the Lager House, or Tiger Stadium to the north to draw crowds like ants to spilled sugar. The Tigers were a magnet for suburbanites, who'd line their Cadillacs and Cutlasses up and down Michigan Avenue, the money bursting the seams in their pockets. My family inherited a parking lot on Trumbull, but that well ran dry when after a century of major-league ball in our neighborhood the Tigers just trotted off, leaving behind a sad and hulking mess that nobody wants. The stadium's still there, nine years later, a painful reminder of a better life, though out of loyalty or homage it's the only abandoned building on Michigan that isn't carved up, burned out, or sprayed with State Boyz and Plato tags.

Listen, I'm not going to get nostalgic; I'm not going to bend your ear about the heyday when bleacher creatures and CEOs wanted the same thing–warm hot dogs, cold beer, and a major-league pennant–or how Michigan Avenue suddenly popped bright when the outfield lights snapped on. I could see them from my bedroom window; I could hear the crack of the bat and I always pretended it was Kaline or Horton, the guys my father said were heroes, giving the opposing team pure hell. Why am I telling you this? Because, after the depot closed, people's low-level fear turned into full-on panic when Tiger Stadium shut down, when Corktown's seemingly sturdy bookends fell, crushing us under their collective weight. People grew sad when they realized they could no longer describe the boundaries of their city as anything within a one-mile radius of the pitcher's mound, and they grew hopeless when they watched Reedy's and the Gold Dollar get nailed up tight, graffiti-splattered boards covering multipaned antique windows crafted by their Irish ancestors nearly two hundred years before. People change when they watch their heritage being obliterated, when they walk past vacant buildings every day, when they feel the luster fading from their lives. They do desperate things. I'm not making excuses for Mrs. O'Leary; I'm just telling you how it was.

When our Trumbull lot closed I was out of a job, which was bittersweet for my father, who didn't care for his twenty-two-year-old daughter collecting money in parking lots but who could also cast his eyes across the cars and calculate the night's take in mere seconds. For a while I just kicked around Detroit, thinking with my associate degree in business administration I might get a part-time office job in the Fisher Building, hopefully near the top floors so I could watch the peregrine falcons loop and dive into the chaos below. What did they see from their sky-top perches? Not the smoke from the Seven Sisters; those stacks had been detonated three years before in '96. I wondered what the falcons thought of the sixteen-story dust cloud that turned their daytime sky dark for three full minutes after the Hudson's Building on Woodward was imploded two years later. Then I realized that what they thought mattered about as much as what I did.

Jefferson Avenue looked so much brighter than Michigan Avenue as I traipsed along in my mid-heeled shoes, resumé tucked into the small briefcase my father used on insurance calls. Why was I relieved when told I was overqualified for the receptionist's job at the ad agency in the Ren Cen, when DuMouchelles said they'd prefer to hire someone with knowledge of Royal Doulton pottery, when the dental office in the Fisher Building never called back? My father said I'd been ruined for indoor work, that working outside even in inclement weather beats the hell out of typing letters in the nicest office. He was right. At night I'd sometimes walk to the lot for old times' sake, past the Corktown houses with their crumbling Queen Anne turrets, Georgian Revival roof lines, Greek columns—what were the city planners thinking? Things that were once charming became irritating. The antique buildings felt old and lifeless, the formerly vibrant skyline a jagged silhouette in the pre-night dusk, the family-owned bars a haven for punk and goth wannabes, their pink rubber mini-skirts and chain-draped leather dresses hiked up for the jump onto handmade mahogany barstools. The bars that were trying to weather the economic storm—LJ's, Casey's Pub, the Parabox—did it by offering dirt-cheap drink specials, and kids sporting neck corsets, rhinestone sunglasses and platform boots studded with more straps and buckles than a straitjacket would sweep through Corktown for a quick buzz before moving on to the night's real adventure at St. Andrew's or City Club. They wrapped their tattooed hands around the brass bar rail, slipped their studded tongues into the tall pilsner glasses, and we felt violated. They were the dark infiltration of the outside world. Part of me understood—I was young, I went to college with kids like this, I saw their need to be provocative—but the timing was just bad. Everything was falling apart, and they seemed to be leading the charge. Well, hustler Mike Ilitch and Mayor Dennis Archer had led the charge, and the painted and hole-punched kids, like entitled vultures, picked at the carrion in their wake.

My loyalty to Detroit and the fact that the intermittent classes I was taking at Wayne State weren't going to pay for themselves led me to O'Leary's Tearoom at Brooklyn and Porter, where I took a job waiting tables and reading tarot cards in the afternoons for rich ladies from West Bloomfield or Northville who had nothing better to do than seek out the novelty of a town that they were too dim or too dismissive to see was drowning before their eyes. They lifted the homemade shortbread to their lips with soft, tanned hands and tapped manicured nails against off-white china cups as they sipped Irish Breakfast tea while waiting their turn at the tarot table. Mrs. O'Leary was the true psychic, though, had worked hard to teach me the cards herself, but she never read for these women. She served their scones and muffins with a fake smile, poured their tea while exchanging pleasantries, but later she would say what small, sad lives they lived, that she couldn't read for them because she'd have to tell the truth. "Honesty Above All Else" was her motto, and the motto of her mother and her mother's mother ad infinitum, traveling in the minds and sensibilities of the O'Leary women from across the Atlantic, remaining intact all the way from County Cork. The words, in Gaelic, had been carved into a wooden plaque and hung over the front door of the tearoom. Locals can handle it, she said, the Irish are strong, practical, resilient. But if she told these women the truth, they'd never come back, and then where would we be? That's why I read for them. It wasn't that I didn't believe in the truth, I just wasn't a good enough psychic to see it. What I saw clearly were the women's designer clothes and leather shoes, their diamond-studded watches and sharp haircuts, and their lives didn't look small to me. But, as I said, I was never able to see the things that Mrs. O'Leary did. Telling this story now makes me miss everything: the weed-smothered Trumbull lot, Tiger Stadium glowing like an earthbound constellation, the tearoom with its lace doilies and antique spoons, Mrs. O'Leary with her black tooth and her visions of misery.

She did not see good things in Detroit's future; she said she dreamed of flood waters gushing over the banks of the Detroit

River, a tidal wave as tall as Cobo Hall consuming Grand Circus Park, then fanning eastward to smother Greektown and westward to our very doors, water rising to overtake the front steps of Corktown's crumbling worker's cottages. She stared at the window as if she could see the nightmare being projected there, fingering the Celtic cross over her breast, her eyes far, far away. "There was a torrent on Porter," she said, "and we were in it, you and me, the tearoom gone, my china cups bobbing around like corks." After noticing my horrified expression, she smiled. "Ah!" she said. "It's this casino stuff's got me riled up."

Despite the fact that citizens had twice voted against it, the mayor had just granted a license to MGM to build a casino in Detroit, and Mrs. O'Leary said she'd be damned to hell and roasted crisp before she sat back and let that happen. "They're all crooked," she'd spat, the *Free Press* and *Detroit Monthly* spread across the table before her. "Politicians steal our money and give it to these greed-mongers. This one's taking bribes, that one's wife's having an affair. What do they care as long as they can build their casino? Come here and look at what they're doing to your city." She made me read about the latest political graft or look at the smug grin of a socialite newly arrived on Detroit's small glamour circuit. "Look at that," she'd say, poking her chubby finger into the face of the offender, her tone bursting with rancor. I'd scuttle into the kitchen or hide in the alcove behind the china cabinet while polishing the silver when she was in one of her dark moods, when she cursed the politicians, the casino owners, the people of Detroit themselves, who she worried would grow apathetic and allow themselves to be steamrolled by corruption. This is when she'd pull out the White Pages, address an envelope in her looping cursive and drop her business card inside, and I'd wonder who was on the receiving end of her selective advertising. But she wrote many letters: to her family back in Cork, to the newspapers, to watchdog groups, to the mayor's office. Though I was young, my future not necessarily tied to Detroit, even I understood her anger over its recent state, her worry over the fate of her business. Mrs. O'Leary, for her part, was convinced that if the MGM people knew how desperate the people of Detroit were—*Who's going to put $50 down on a blackjack table? They'll come in and rob the place, that's what they'll do*!—they would thank the mayor kindly and be on their way.

"Go read their tarot," I said. "Tell them they'll be sorry."

"You can laugh," she countered, "but these businessmen wouldn't bring their families here if they knew how dangerous it was. They wouldn't want to open a casino if something happened to stop them. And this is a place where bad things happen." She nodded knowingly, but I laughed at her naïveté, for I wasn't too young to know that there's no stopping the push of capitalism. Actually the casino was just the latest impediment in her drive to save Detroit: she was working to have Archer impeached, the new Tiger Stadium—she would not say the words "Comerica Park"—boycotted, and Mike Ilitch run out on a rail.

This is the history of the story I'm trying to tell you, the thing that happened in the tearoom, the thing I can tell you now that Mrs. O'Leary is dead. All that fear and sadness drove Mrs. O'Leary to do what she did, but who's to say that under similar pressure you wouldn't have done the same thing?

It should not surprise you, then, that he appeared before us on a desperate night, for there were many desperate nights in Corktown after the close of the '99 season. Perhaps I should have taken as portents what I dismissed simply as the manifestations of a dying city as I walked to work that day: a man running down Church with a pair of crutches under his arm, a woman pushing a baby stroller full of empty bottles, a car without a passenger door cruising slowly up Leverette. That night the sleet was driving down, little needles piercing the gray snow below, and even though the tart smell of cabbage was making me queasy, the drone of the rain and the six-block walk home kept me there long after I should have left, flipping cards in a Hearts and Spades game against my employer. We were on display at Mrs. O'Leary's favorite linen-covered table in the front window of the tearoom, which always made me feel like a target at night, but Mrs. O'Leary seemed oblivious to the paranoia of a fearful mind. Is it an indictment of Mrs. O'Leary's psychic ability to say that when the doorbell chimed we both gasped? Why? Because we hadn't expected anyone, of course; we couldn't imagine anyone strolling around in the knife-like torrent. But there he was.

The man who stood before us looked as if he'd just walked out of a movie—chiseled features, dripping trench coat, a brown fedora. We stared at him, and Mrs. O'Leary said, "I'll get the tea."

"That's all right," he said. "I don't need any tea."

"Yes, you do," she said. "Sit down."

The man–he couldn't have known, the cards weren't out–sat at the tarot table, far from the dark front windows. "My car broke down on Bagley," he said as Mrs. O'Leary placed a teacup before him, and by the way she smiled, showing only the lower left corner of her blackened tooth, I knew she didn't believe him. Though she had a stockpot of food warming in the kitchen, she never offered him any—do you see what I mean about the way she knew things?

The man took a small sip of his tea and smiled. Later, I'd learn that she'd put two fingers of Ballantine's in his cup, that she knew he needed it, and you didn't have to be a psychic to see that he was grateful. Mrs. O'Leary nodded at me then, as if we'd earlier set up a system of communication that would tell me exactly what to do, but my psychic abilities, as usual, had failed. Though she'd been teaching me the tarot for two months, I still struggled. I knew the meaning of the cards—I'd memorized them as easily as I'd mentally charted who owned each car in the Trumbull lot—but when I had to transplant their meanings into the lives of the people who sat before me, their fear and exhilaration always seemed to short-circuit my intuition. She nodded again, then turned to the man, who had removed his hat to reveal a thick head of red-blond hair, and said, "Why don't you have your tarot read while you wait?"

He looked at her expectantly, as if that is precisely why he'd come, as if she'd read his mind. I recall thinking that I had read his mind too, just then, that my skills had kicked in, that my intuitive antennae were finally picking up signals from the psychic airwaves around me. I was suddenly convinced that he had come to us deliberately, desperately, and I knew then that I would be the one to save this poor soul, this gorgeous man. Is arrogance not the downfall of the fool? Before Mrs. O'Leary could stand up I had stationed myself across from him and pulled the tarot pack from its green silk pouch. That she believed me incapable of doing any real harm seemed clear when she poured herself three fingers of Ballantine's and pretended to read Thomas Lemurra's bestseller *The Boneyard Will Wait* at the small table where I had been losing all night. Perhaps that was yet another missed sign.

"All right, then," I said to the man before turning on the tape recorder. "For five dollars you can buy a tape of the reading." This was something the rich ladies loved, for they'd often repeat the same questions, their recall apparently faulty.

Mrs. O'Leary, her back to us, sighed heavily and shook her head, and the man stared at me like I was insane. He then shrugged out of his wet coat and draped it over a vacant chair beside us, and I imagined I could smell the taunting rain and bitter smoke in its folds, the fear that seeped into my nostrils like ammonia. I started turning cards immediately after he'd cut them, eager, too eager, I see now, to test my newfound skills.

The first card was the two of Wands, a lone, lost man with his back turned, the card of mortification. This card meant that the man before me had received news, bad news. Next came the Empress, crowned in stars and robed in gold, signaling his involvement with a strong, wealthy woman, but isn't that common among handsome men? At any rate, I turned the third card, a reversed Ace of Pentacles, a gargantuan hand clutching an oversized coin and symbolizing the dark side of wealth.

"You've had some bad luck," I said, hoping for some acknowledgment from him, but he was like a stone. I turned more cards: The four of Cups, an inconsolable man, then the two of Pentacles: fear, obstacles, romantic entanglement.

"There is a woman," I said. "She is raven-haired. She is powerful. She is tormented." Of course, I didn't know for certain that the woman in charge of his troubles was raven-haired—only Mrs. O'Leary would know *that*—but I think it was a safe bet that a woman was at the root of his unhappiness, for my father had always said that a woman is at the root of most men's unhappiness, and I had a one in four shot at getting hair color right. His tension was wreaking havoc on my psychic radar, and it shut down entirely when he whispered his first question: "Is she going to kill me?"

The women from Grosse Pointe and Bingham Farms never asked questions like this. They wanted to know if their husbands would be promoted, if their sons would get into Yale, if they would be safe under the scalpel during plastic surgery. I turned the seven of Cups, which is merely a dark child. "Not yet," I said. "Maybe never."

Next came the eight of Cups, the child growing. "But she's thinking about it." How else can one read that sequence? Mrs. O'Leary, God rest her soul, was no help at all, staring into the abyss framed by the window and humming "Danny Boy" while thumbing the handle on her Prince Albert china cup.

The reversed Queen of Swords was next. It had to be the woman. "She's here," I tapped the card, recalling the textbook definition in the *Pictorial Key to the Tarot*: "This queen has intentions that, in the reversed position, cannot be exercised."

The man looked from me to the card and back again, frowning.

"She's upside-down," I said. "Immobilized. Her sword is useless in this position."

He tilted his head. "I see," he said, absently running his fingers along the belt of the trench coat beside him before downing his remaining tea. *What did he see?* I wondered, and I had to stop myself from asking.

I then turned the King of Swords, handsome, troubled, the least wealthy of the four kings.

"This is you," I said. Who else could it be?

"And?"

And I was blank. Nothing. "And you're in some kind of trouble." It was an idiotic thing to say—you didn't need a tarot pack to figure that out—but it was also safe. Was I in over my head? Should I have summoned Mrs. O'Leary out of what I thought was her liquor-induced complacency, ended the reading right there? Of course, but there's no use in posing those questions now, though on the blackest nights I often do.

I next turned the six of Pentacles, prosperity, followed by the Knight of Pentacles, more prosperity, and then I sat there staring at the cards as if the characters on them would speak, waiting for something to happen. And then it did.

"This Knight of Pentacles," Mrs. O'Leary croaked from across the room, "is your queen's husband. A dangerous man."

"But he's not a king," the man argued.

I stared at the cards, the King of Swords lying beside the upside-down Queen of Swords on the table. "You're her king," she answered, "without a kingdom."

I remained silent and next turned the ten of Swords. Let me make it clear that no one told me to do that. No one told me to turn another card, but I did.

Mrs. O'Leary gasped, and we turned to her. At the time it meant little to me, but now, before I take my sleeping pills, before I ask myself why I didn't walk out of the tearoom and not look back, before I blame the closing of the stadium for what transpired, the vision of Mrs. O'Leary, a smirk stretching the bottom of her face, haunts me. The man knew, even if he didn't know for certain, what even I could see: that this was the card of horrific death.

"What is it?"

"Nothing," I said.

"He's on the ground with swords in his back. That doesn't look like nothing," he said. "Tell me."

"It's bad." I stared at him. "I see the raven-haired woman." And I did. Was it the night? Was it the sudden appearance of this troubled man in this troubled neighborhood with his questions of death that triggered a vision clearer than if she'd been standing before me in the flesh? I saw her, or I called her up from some deep place of knowing: a thick bowl of black hair sprouting from a sharp widow's peak, blunt red talons, a smile like a blade in her teeth. "It's bad," I repeated.

"Yes," he said, leaning back in his chair and setting his chin like a man about to take a punch. He stared at the cards intently, almost as if he could read them. "It's bad."

My heart constricted, and I understood for the first time the true depth of Mrs. O'Leary's burden: how could she channel all this pain and heartache? No wonder she drank Ballantine's, no wonder her tooth had rotted from the toxic news that had washed over it each time she read a tarot. My head was pounding, and I had to remind myself to breathe. "Maybe this is enough for now," I said.

The man nodded at the deck in my hand, and as I slowly turned the next card, an upside-down knight wielding a large gray sword, Mrs. O'Leary said, "The reversed Knight of Swords spells doom. Do you want another card?"

The man nodded again, and it was then that I realized how little he'd spoken that night.

Mrs. O'Leary was staring at the plaque above the door, her jaw set, her back rigid. She could not have seen the cards from where she sat, even with her glasses on, but as I turned the most feared card in the tarot, the skeleton coming to claim on his white horse, she said, "Death may not be imminent, but it is present."

"I know," he sighed. "I know."

Next came the six of Swords, the symbol of painful journey, and I dared not recite the definition of the card as it appeared in this sequence: "Your death will be violent." But I didn't have to, because Mrs. O'Leary did.

Mrs. O'Leary was never comfortable telling clients that tarot readings are for entertainment purposes only, that they are not to be considered financial, legal, or psychological counseling, but we always did. And that's what she told the detectives who showed up at O'Leary's three days after the skeleton slipped the tape into the pocket of his trench coat and threw a fifty on the table.

"I heard on the news," she said. "But I can't help you."

"Well, you can't claim client privilege," said the elderly detective in a cheap suit as he pulled the tape from his briefcase and slid it across the table. "Who's the other voice on the tape? Doesn't sound like you."

"It's mine," she said, "there's no one else here does tarot. It's a cheap tape, bad quality."

Through a crack in the saloon doors that opened onto the kitchen I watched the detectives exchange looks.

"It was just a wee bit of fun," said Mrs. O'Leary with badly played nonchalance. "He came in to get out of the weather."

"Well, it doesn't sound very funny to me," said the detective with the acid-trip necktie. "Does it sound funny to you?" he asked Cheap Suit, who shook his head.

"See that? Neither of us find it funny. Maybe we lack a sense of humor, but we don't find murder funny."

When I saw Mrs. O'Leary crumple to the chair before enlisting a phony brogue, I wanted to rush out of the kitchen and take the blame for something horrible, something I didn't yet fully understand, for a death I could have prevented. But I didn't.

"Sounds to me like Mr. Donegan felt he was going to be killed," said Necktie as he stared at the tape. "Now how do you suppose he came to that conclusion?"

"Aye, he knew it when he walked in, lad."

"You sure didn't help matters."

"I'm not here to alter fate," said Mrs. O'Leary.

"Did Donegan say anything you didn't get on this tape?"

"No."

"Are you sure?"

"As me great-grandmother used to say, 'He wasn't the talkin' sort.'"

"Well, his trap's sure zipped now," said Cheap Suit.

"We found this in his coat pocket," said Necktie as he held up a small white business card. "Where do you suppose he got it?"

"Me cards are there on the table," said Mrs. O'Leary, nodding. "Who's to say?"

Necktie then unfolded the front-page *Free Press* article describing the murder of Victoria Lanni, the wife of MGM casino chairman CEO Terrance Lanni, with a tiny corner photograph of her very handsome killer, Bruce Donegan.

"Maybe," he said, "this will jar your memory."

She stared at the photograph, then touched it. "Nothing," she said.

"So he thought Mrs. Lanni was going to kill him," said Cheap Suit as he wiped his eye with a yellowed handkerchief. "Why do you think she'd do a thing like that?"

Mrs. O'Leary shrugged.

The detectives glanced at each other. "You never saw him killing her?" said Necktie, and I felt Mrs. O'Leary staring at me through the thick wooden door, her voice softening to a whisper.

"I just saw death," she said.

"Strangulation?" said Necktie. "Trench coat belt?"

"No. Dirtier, nastier. I don't know what. And I saw it on him. All over him."

"Well, you're good then," said Cheap Suit. "Because Lanni's got some dark pals in prison."

When the detectives left I rushed from the kitchen to find Mrs. O'Leary still seated at her favorite table near a pile of magazines she'd quickly gathered when she saw them enter.

"I only needed *her* dead," said Mrs. O'Leary, "so her husband would pack up his poker chips and his blackjack tables and leave." She shook her head.

She shifted the papers before her, and that's when the image assaulted me. That's when I saw the article I'd read the month before only to satisfy her, the one in which casino chairman Terrance Lanni's wife denies having an affair with handsome local Bruce Donegan, the one that speculates she will lose her fortune if the affair is confirmed, the one that's wrapped around a color photo of a woman with a thick bowl of black hair sprouting from a sharp widow's peak, blunt red talons, a smile like a blade in her teeth.

Did Mrs. O'Leary know that the following month Terrance Lanni would resign as MGM Grand's CEO after his wife was strangled in their Riverfront Towers apartment, that Bruce Donegan would bleed to death in a dark corner of the prison's laundry room after being stabbed twenty-six times? "It was bound to happen" was all she'd say, though I still wonder if things would have been different had I not turned that fateful card, if I'd refused to continue the reading, left my post at the table and ran home under a black sky that would bleed ice for the next two days. If, if, if. Despite her visions and machinations to save Detroit, the following year Mrs. O'Leary's tearoom closed as the casinos opened, and she packed her china sets and her wooden plaque for the long journey back to Cork.

Her obituary said she was a member of the Gaelic League and a secretary of the local Preservation Society, known for the cuisine she served at her long-term Irish tearoom in Corktown. "She will be missed," the article stated, "for her kindness, her generosity and her willingness to help everyone who crossed her doorstep." Mrs. O'Leary died yesterday, and today I can tell a different story.

reaping

Her hair was pulled up into a plastic bag and red dye trickled down her face and neck as she stood on the front porch trembling. "Do you see this?" she yelled, pointing to her face. "This is anger. A-N-G-E-R. You better get your goddamn asses in here right now, Kate, or I swear to God, my head'll explode. I swear to *God*." I was only six, but that was old enough to be embarrassed by the neighborhood kids' laughter as I grabbed Stinky's hand and dragged him up the stairs and past our mother, all the while keeping a close watch on her head. My brother's real name is Nicky but we called him Stinky because he usually packed a full diaper. Nicky, who was only two, laughed at our mother's antics, pointed at her red-splattered face. He wouldn't understand humiliation for a long time.

I LIVE IN AN APARTMENT on East Seventeenth and work for a large investment firm. I put in long hours and work most weekends, but I don't mind. I dated a lawyer for a while, and I learned that lawyers are too serious. They want to talk about the future, they want to talk about the past. In short, they're busybodies. I couldn't live with someone like that so I broke it off. I'm a private person: I go to the museum in my spare time, I read books and play with my cats. But I'm not one of *those*; I don't dress them up and let them eat at the dining room table, for chrissake.

I ALWAYS WORRIED ABOUT NICKY when I was at school, imagining him wandering out of the house to get kidnapped by a child molester or hit by a speeding car while Mama slept. Mama read the notes Mrs. Lesch pinned to my jacket and said, "Why aren't you paying attention in class? What the hell's wrong with you? Are you one of those AED kids or somethin'? I can't afford to take you to no goddamn sociopath doctor." She rubbed her temples. "I swear to *God* this head's gonna pop right off." I told her I could do better. "Not if you inherited your bastard father's brains you won't." I promised I would shape up. "Oh, you *will*," she said. "You see this?" She pointed to her face. "This is anger."

Nicky is a shipping clerk for a small catalog distributor in Idaho. He finally sold his house and bought a condo because he was tired of lawn work and thought maybe he'd start dating if he had more time. We see each other often, although I usually travel because Nicky is afraid to fly. Last time I visited I took some pastries I'd bought from Stella's around the corner but regretted it the moment I saw Nicky's hungry eyes glaring above a stomach that spilled over his belt. "You've put on weight," I said, tightening my grip on the bakery box. "Just a little," he said, wrestling it away and digging in.

The house smelled like food when I got home from school, so I knew that Mama must have been in a good mood. Nicky, who as usual sat in front of the sofa banging his head against the cushion, jumped up to greet me. "Boom!" he said and ran into the kitchen. The cupboards, walls and floor were splattered with thick green slime, and Nicky stomped his feet in puddles of it. I found out later that Mama had been cooking pea soup in her pressure cooker when she passed out and the lid blew. Meanwhile I searched the kitchen for her headless body, certain that this was the long-awaited event.

My boss said I had to take a vacation, that I was accruing too much time and the company wouldn't pay me for it. I told everyone at the office that I was going to Aruba with a man I'd met at a Goya exhibit, a visiting art professor from Brazil. I then loaded up on groceries and liquor, library books and movies before going home and calling Nicky. "Hey, Stinky," I said to his answering machine, "I guess you're out on a hot date. Call me when you get home." He called after midnight and said that he and a friend from Weight Watchers had gone to an arcade after their meeting. "You're thirty-three, Nicky. Arcade?" He sighed. "Kate? Have you been drinking?" Nicky thinks his microscopic scrutiny of our mother's drinking problem makes him an expert on alcoholism. "No," I lied. A few shots of Cuervo, at least to me, doesn't constitute drinking. Technically, I was vacationing in Aruba anyway.

I SHOULD HAVE DONE SOMETHING when he slapped Nicky. I was seven, and that's old enough to know better. Mama met him at the corner bar; she'd sprained her ankle slipping off a barstool and he, in princely fashion, carried her home. She, kicking her legs, and he, howling and staggering, were a barely mobile ruckus clamoring down Frankel Street. The next morning when Nicky refused to eat his cereal and the prince backhanded him out of his chair, I didn't say anything. Instead I grabbed Nicky, who was crying more from shock than pain, and dragged him to his room where I did something I should have done long before. "Guess what?" I said. "We're gonna change your diaper."

"HER NAME IS SHELBY. SHE sounds bubbly," Nicky said when he told me about the woman who'd answered his personal ad. "She said she's not exactly pretty and not exactly small, has short blond hair, likes romance novels. She's not perfect but, hey, look at me," he laughed. "You're a terrific guy, Nick. Don't sell yourself short." Silence. "I'm afraid, Kate. Afraid to meet her, afraid not to meet her, afraid of the disappointed look." My heart skipped. "Do you want me to fly out?" Without missing a beat, he said, "Okay. I love you."

The check was late. We were eating oatmeal for dinner again, which was fine with Nicky and me because Mama let us draw pictures on top with Hershey syrup. But Mama was angry. "Bet Leland's eating a steak right now. He'll broil in hell in his own fat. All landlords are goin' to hell," she said. "Bet they don't teach *that* in school." Nicky shook his head with authority; he was in second grade. Mama's pacing was punctuated by glances through the front window; she was lying in wait for the mailman. She assumed her battle position on the front porch and started shouting when she spotted him up the block. "You better have my check, you stupid bastard. And you better put it right here." She poked her left palm with her right index finger. "Right here. Move your lazy ass!" The mailman, evidently unimpressed by Mama's theatrics, presented several flyers and a gas bill. "No check," he said, holding his right hand in the Stop position. "I know, I know," he said, "your head's gonna pop off."

I've had nightmares for years, no big deal, but the most recent ones are odd. I fall asleep behind the balustrade in the Impressionist Room at the museum and wake to a gala featuring Toulouse-Lautrec's can-can dancers, spinning, twirling dervishes that sweep me into the fray and taunt me, laugh at my business suit, my odd haircut. An empty frame hangs in place of the *Dance at the Moulin Rouge*, and I understand what's happening when I see Bazille's *Black Woman with Peonies* leave her flower arrangement to step gingerly from her frame onto the marble dance floor. "*Pour vous*," she says, tossing me a pink flower before running to *Le Figaro* and snatching the paper from the reading woman's hands. "*Oubliez le journal!*" she yells. "*Dansez!*" The woman waves her off. "*Je suis fatiguée*," she says before removing her glasses and rubbing her eyes. I usually wake up exhausted. "At least you have a night life," jokes my colleague Janie, who recommends I see a shrink. "Shrinks are for nuts," I say, to which she responds, "So what's your point?"

Mama's head hadn't popped off by the time Nicky was nine, so in what seemed like an effort to accelerate the event, he started swearing at school. "I'll kill the little bastard," she said as she slammed down the phone. "Leave him alone," I said. "He's just a kid imitating what he hears—in class." She stroked my hair. This always made me nervous. "You're a good girl," she said. "You know I've had a hard life, don't you?" The liquor had softened her up; at least Nicky wouldn't get it when he got home. "Your father never gave me a stinking rotten cent." She was snoring into the plastic tablecloth when Nicky walked in. "Cool it with your mouth, sport," I said. "School called." He stared at the back of her head and said, "She go bat shit?"

Nicky left to meet his blind date and I searched his place for liquor. Not a drop. I cleaned instead, to distract myself but also to take care of my brother, to celebrate his big night. I found empty chip bags under the bed, half-eaten pretzels under cushions and candy bar wrappers in the bathroom trash. I knew I'd have to mention it, but I wasn't sure how to approach him. I had told Nicky about my dreams, thinking we'd both have a good laugh, but he just sighed. He'd been gone little more than an hour when I heard his key in the lock. "Don't worry, Kate, it's only me," he called through the door, then walked in all smiles, balancing a pizza box on his arm. "What happened?" I asked. "Nothing. I guess she couldn't make it." He shrugged. "I'm sorry, honey," I said. "What kind of name is Shelby anyway?" He pushed up his glasses, held out the pizza and said, "Hungry?"

Mama and Nicky were waltzing around the kitchen when I got home from school, she in a green chiffon dress and heels and he in a baseball cap and fake Converse All Stars. "What gives?" I asked. "This is the big one," said Mama, "a plumber. We'll be on easy street if I play it right. Don't wait up. There's macaroni and cheese in the fridge." Nicky grimaced and said, "Not that shit again." Mama waited by the front door, drinking and staring at the street until the phone rang. "You're *what*?" she cried before slamming down the receiver. She took a deep breath, released it slowly. "You two sit there and close your eyes." I recall the rustling of chiffon as she flitted around the kitchen opening drawers, her warnings to keep our eyes closed and the whisper of air escaping the plastic cushion as she plopped onto a kitchen chair. But what I remember best is Nicky screaming "Sonofabitch, sonofabitch, sonofabitch" after she inserted the gun into her right ear and pulled the trigger.

My shrink attributes my nightmares to fear, anxiety, pent-up anger from the past, blah, blah, blah. They all blame your parents. So my mother was a drunk. No one has a perfect childhood. He wants to do regressive hypnotherapy, wants me to come in *twice* a week, bloodsucking bastard. I tell him it's job pressure, that my projects are falling behind because of our appointments, that it's my boss and not my mother stressing me out by making these visits a condition of my employment. I should have stayed home, but the merger report was due, so I slipped the brandy into my briefcase and took only a few swigs during lunch to fight my cold. I was dizzy from fever when I tripped on a plastic runner, banging my briefcase against a partition wall as I fell, sending its contents sailing halfway across the office. The brandy bottle bounced twice across the ceramic tile before crashing into the molding outside my supervisor's door. Janie has taken over some of my clients and lied to them about my absences, but my colleagues cast sympathy stares, stop talking when I enter the room.

The Pierces were much nicer than our first foster parents, but we blew it. I couldn't get Nicky to do his homework, and Mrs. Pierce got calls from most of his teachers saying he ignored them in class. When he accidentally set his bed on fire, she said we had to go.

She didn't say it to us, but I heard her talking to Social Services. "I feel horrible," she said, "those poor children. But I'm not trained to handle pathological kids. I don't know what to do with him." Well, there was nothing wrong with Nicky, and that's what I told our case worker. "If you send him to the nuthouse you might as well send us both because he's no crazier than I am." We moved through many foster homes but felt lucky to stay together.

New Year's Eve, 11:59 p.m. Nicky and I are at his condo. I'm watching him eat ribs left over from dinner and feel guilty when he says "I'll diet next year" because I am cradling a tumbler of vodka he thinks is water. As the ball begins its slow descent, I take Nicky's hand, I tell him next year will be better. Gunfire erupts at midnight, and I hold Nicky as he covers his ears and weeps.

tom hanks wants a story: the anatomy of a tale

So, let's say Tom Hanks asks you to write a story that he can turn into a movie. You meet him at Starbucks in your home town where he's shooting a crime thriller and tell him you're a writer in an understated way and you don't bug him and you're not obnoxious so he takes a liking and says, *How about you write me a story, Jenna Crump? I'm going to give you my email address. I don't want you to abuse my email address, Jenna Crump, but I'm going to give it to you and when you write a story I can make into a movie you send it over to me. I don't expect it in a day or in a week and I won't even be waiting for it but when you finish it you send it over.*

So right now, this very minute, while Tom Hanks is not waiting for you to send him a story he can make into a movie you should be able to write, uninhibited and pressure-free, write until the cocks crow and the cows come home. Tom Hanks is officially not waiting for you to send him a story, but your agent is. Your agent believes you will send *him* a story and another one and another one and even the novel you promised; he's so confident, in fact, that he doesn't bug you about it, doesn't check in, doesn't demand progress reports. Often you think he's just given up, but you convince yourself that he is patient, understands your need for space, knows how deeply rooted and dependable your talent is—in these respects your agent is like your mother. Tom Hanks would not be this patient, not if he were waiting for something. Why should he be? But he is not waiting, and this is why it is the perfect time to write the story he is not waiting for.

What will you write about? Your agent loved your last story about the pet lizard that is set free. "Write another one like that," he said. "I could do that," you said, knowing that you never would. Why would you want to write the same story? Nobody does that but Stephen King. Me, I get bored. If my agent only knew how bored I get, how lazy I usually am, how much more creative I am in coming up with excuses not to write than in my actual writing. He's a good guy just trying to make a living off my sweat (and the sweat of writers who actually write). That's why agents need multiple authors—except, I guess, for Stephen King's agent. Our output is erratic, dictated by so many variables it would certainly boggle the mind of the less creative person. When one author is down another must surely be up. Woe to the author who is up, I say, for you know what's coming.

So now that Tom Hanks is not waiting for a story I will dish something up: talking fish, wunderkind Sudoku champion, zombies in the heartland, zombies in the grocery, zombies in my bed. That could work. That's what I tell my students: "Surprise me. Don't offer up the expected: I don't want shuffling zombies, flesh-eating zombies or dim-witted zombies." The zombies I received from the students in my creative writing workshop pillage tomato gardens, coach soccer teams, work as crossing guards. What did I do wrong? I did not steer them clear of *boring* zombies. People in these stories were sharing buses, park benches and taxis with zombies, oblivious to their, well, *zombieism.* Maybe this was a philosophical comment about contemporary America, about which I have this to say: Zombies are a hackneyed metaphor for the state of the modern psyche. So that's how I decide to write a zombie story for Tom Hanks, one that's not been written before, one that is not boring, and one that does not rely for its effect on cultural philosophizing. Where to begin? At the end, of course.

The city is in flames. No, the city is not in flames. In fact, all is peaceful, or at least there is a prevailing sense of equilibrium. No, that's no hook. There is a hand. I think Stephen King started one of his books with this line, therefore there is no hand. But there is a man in the garden, which I know is inspired by the zombie pillaging tomatoes story, but be patient. There is a man in a garden repeatedly stabbing at a stubborn root, and there is something awkward in his motion; perhaps he's tired, or lost in thought, or something else. He's wearing a flannel shirt unevenly buttoned so that a small triangle of material hangs down in front, the corner catching the updraft each time he slumps down to slam the hoe into solid oak. The root does not give. He stops and listens to the sound of nothing, his mouth dry, then begins another vigorous cycle of slump and slam. The root does not give. His breathing remains shallow as he drops the garden tool and limps toward the back door of the house, touching the creeper vines that grow into a flowery wall across the trellis, pausing at the first step to clutch his meaty thigh between his hands and lift his numb leg onto the first cement stair. Then he hears them, their monotonous drone like a thousand bees descending, a low-decibel siren, a choir of baffled notes in the same pitch. He stands for a moment on the top stair, his pale hands gripping his left thigh, before yanking his leg to the second stair, the third. The voices don't worry him, for they are always and everywhere now, and he knows that they will not come for him.

Is this because he's a zombie? That's what I thought at first with the awkward motion and the slumping, the leg dragging. But then I thought that maybe he was hurt by the zombies and he is felling the tree to make a protective fire. And if this were the case, I thought that he knew they wouldn't come for him because he'd been alone and afraid for so long that he wanted to die. So, of course, they wouldn't come because zombies never do what you want them to do. Then I thought that they *should* come for him since it's what the protagonist wants, so these zombies would be acting out of stereotype, at least in this story. Then I considered the most important angle: what would Tom Hanks think? I mean, he's not a zombie-movie guy that I know of, but he wanted a story and not a script and never mentioned anything about being cast himself. He said, *When you write a story I can make into a movie, you send it over.* You ask me, that's a pretty open-ended request. So what type of zombie would Tom Hanks like? I don't know, but surely it's got to be an original zombie, a compelling zombie, a zombie of mythic proportion. Or maybe not. Maybe he wants a relatable zombie. It is important to note here that relatable and boring are not the same thing. Because we can relate to the zombie does not mean that his story will be overly familiar, which is one step away from being boring. So, think about this: what if a zombie had suddenly shown up on the allegedly uninhabited island Tom Hanks occupies in *Castaway*? Obviously you'd have an entirely different movie there. What if Tom Hanks was trying to forestall the execution of a psychic zombie in *The Green Mile*? Maybe Forrest Gump's wheelchair-bound buddy is a zombie. A zombie on a shrimp boat. Which begs the question: Can zombies swim? Or, more particularly, can paralyzed zombies swim? I'm pretty sure his friend falls overboard in that movie. Enough.

What I need is one singular zombie: not too familiar, not too bizarre, relatable yet intangible, sympathetic yet . . . creepy. Kind of like my ex-husband.

So our friend in the flannel shirt, his forehead slick with sweat, drags his leg into the house, over the metal threshold which *tink*s when the steel-framed eyelets of his boot strike it. It is a peculiar sound, like a pebble hitting glass or a fingernail flicking an empty can, but he has heard it before and so, like the acrid smell of burnt coffee or the bruised fruit crawling with flies, it does not register. What else does not register? The growing pile of damp mail, fused into a yellow knoll near the front door, the shredded blinds dangling from bent rods above the picture window, the dead cat turned on its side, legs stiffened into an eternal stretch. The dead cat may not distract the main character, but it will distract the reader: was it killed by the zombie-protagonist along with everyone else in the house, or was it starved by its loving but frantic human owner-protagonist who in his zeal to survive forgets to feed his pet, or has the lone-survivor-protagonist, run from his own home, holed up in here with an unknown dead cat? What is the dead cat a metaphor *for*? A bloody cat is a very different thing than an emaciated cat, which is a different thing yet from a beheaded cat. The cat can be a great clue but also a narrative nuisance. So for now I say, kill the cat. Then what happened to the blinds? We will address that later. For now what troubles me is the mail.

The mail is still being delivered during what we must assume to be a zombie invasion. Perhaps the letter carrier is a zombie? Absolutely not. Still, the mail arrives, so the new letter carrier credo must be "Neither cold, nor rain nor sleet nor dark of night nor zombie infestation shall stay this courier from his appointed rounds." That is not clever; I grow uncomfortable when writers try too hard to be clever, and sometimes I even feel sorry for them. The thought of readers feeling sorry for me is unthinkable. So, the new letter carrier credo goes the way of the cat.

My zombie story is falling apart but that's because I'm giving up too easily.

Let's go back into the house. Our protagonist, who should have been named five pages ago as I'm not creating an Everyman character—recall my stance on cultural philosophizing—is bone-tired. The sharp reader will read something into the word *bone*, even though it's not used in a horror context, but that is intentional. So, using his numb leg as a cane, Martin stumps through the house toward the bathroom, dragging his booted foot over the gouged wooden floor before falling against the sink in exhaustion. He remains there, bent, his forehead resting on the cold metal faucet until his breath ceases to feel as if it's ascending the elevator of his throat and stopping at each floor. When he straightens his elbows, which burn from the impotent exertion with the hoe, the top of his head is reflected in the mirror, that ever-useful device, called into service by emerging writers who feel they've stumbled upon a brilliant vehicle for physical description.

With a pale, tremulous hand Martin reaches toward the medicine cabinet, slams his craggy nail into the glass twice before catching the door's thin lip and pulling outward, the rusted hinge whining before depositing several orange-brown flakes into the porcelain sink below. Porcelain suggests a white scrubbed beauty, but this porcelain is peeled so that the black undercoat appears as a chain of dark, flat clouds, and if Martin were a contemplative man he might call up that dark cloud/silver lining platitude and perhaps even mine some hope there, but Martin is tired, resigned, and cannot bear to face himself in the mirror. Of course he reaches for the pills, holds the bottle loose in his palm and knows he will be unable to line up the arrows gouged into the plastic cap and the container.

Will he overdose? Boring. Why place characters into precarious situations only to have them wake up from dreams or kill themselves? My students would say because that is realistic, because that is what life is like. I say, if I want boring I have my own life. Martin will not kill himself on my watch any more than the cat that has been excised from this story killed itself. The bottle of aspirin approaches his snarling mouth and Martin clamps down with his front teeth (which are not dentures and which will not come out, though of course it crossed my mind). He twists. Hard. The ridged cap remains fixed, and the sound as his teeth slide across it is that of a small engine, a growl to match his fierce expression. He closes the mirrored door and for the first time understands that he is desperate. This from his eyes, wide, jaundiced, streaked with small red bolts. He bites down, the cap cracks, and orange caplets explode from the cylinder like bullets. Death imagery, sure. Consider it. The pills are scooped—no, this is no time for passive construction—Martin scoops the pills from the dingy porcelain sink and passes them through his parched lips. They crunch like castanets between his teeth, and the bitter taste of the pills' chalky wombs permeates his mouth. Water, he thinks, and that's when he hears them outside, in the garden.

They are not happily pillaging tomatoes. This would be anticlimactic, a sign that my primary intention is not to tell a complete story about the meaning of one life but to demonstrate for you, the reader, yet again the general futility of hope. In the postmodern story the human protagonist will not be killed as he desires, or if he's a zombie he will not kill as programmed but will instead chew some aspirin in an effort to "cure" himself, and in either case the zombies outside will sate themselves with tomatoes. What is the message there? *That's* what Tom Hanks would ask if I were foolish enough to try to pawn off on him a disjointed, overdetermined narrative with no resolution under the guise of radical art. We will not end a movie with a man chugging aspirin while zombies eat tomatoes outside.

Back in the house Martin cups his right hand under the running faucet and bends his face to the sink, slurping from his palm before pushing himself vertical so that he can swallow. Pain engulfs his skull and he pinches two more aspirin from the sink, swallowing them whole. Martin wants to die, this I now know, so why bother with the aspirin? Because a headache won't kill him, but it still hurts. Many people may want to die, but none want to suffer. Why should Martin be any different? He knows that death by zombie will hurt, but only for a short time. He's heard the truncated screams; he's even tried to time them. Sometimes less than a second. At first this mortified him, and he spent hours imagining the events of those tiny moments: a fist through the heart, a crushed skull, a head torn from its root. Not just a fist through the heart, but the jagged yellow nails like knives carving into the chest wall, hand snapping ribs on its pointed mission to the heart, that determined yet fragile symbol of love. A crushed skull is welcome, he thinks, if the attack comes from behind, the blow solid and sure. But what he prefers is the head torn from its root: here, and then gone, one jolt, as in his mind it can occur no other way. Shall I stop here to paint the myriad ways a head can be severed? Of course not.

Martin trudges from the bathroom, up the hall, past the phantom pyramid of musty mail, the empty space the dead cat once occupied, the shredded blinds now whole, toward the metal threshold at the back door where he stands silently and watches them slump toward him.

Of course, Tom Hanks will want backstory, and the first thing that comes to mind is that Martin is a classical violinist: Beethoven, Delibes, Grieg. His favorite songs are "Pastoral," "Feast of the Clock," and "Elegiac Melodies." Sometimes he holds the Cremonese violin in his trembling hands, admires the craftsmanship, the sleek spruce backboard, the ribs a rich maple, no hint of the hide glue that binds each part of the three-hundred-year-old instrument. Surely, you've realized by now the many hours Martin has spent wondering where to hide the rare Guarnari and its slick ebony bow. He's considered burying it in the garden, but the moisture would surely warp the wood; the attic heat might melt the varnish, and the body might freeze stiff in the cellar, taking on a new shape and resonance after its thaw.

Maybe this isn't the end, he thinks, and so the violin should be saved, for it will sound even sweeter after the seasoning of three more centuries. He'd meant to give the instrument to his son, who'd been struck down by a car and killed when he was eight. The grief was bottomless, and so he fell, and he did not try to stop falling for so long that he spent years clawing back up to the land of the living. Three nights ago he laughed aloud at the irony: his son is dead and he is glad; he rejoined the living only to find himself among the dead. So, it's into the pantry he goes, night after night, to retrieve the wooden angel from behind the molasses and Quaker Oats, to gently stroke the bridge, the fret, the scroll, to imagine the world he once inhabited, the lavish orchestra halls, the conductor's slim baton, the lull and the crescendo.

Some things don't change, zombies or not. Life is lull and crescendo. Lull is hoeing in the garden, popping aspirin, cradling a violin you refuse to insult by playing with shaking hands. Crescendo is a car striking a child, an avocation lost, a zombie tearing into your left calf. Suspense is wondering how long before you kill or are killed. When they no longer enter the garden, arms outstretched, and trudge toward you, you've become one of them. Once you fit in, you've lost your appeal. In other words, you're boring. Martin takes pills to kill himself but his body does not respond: this is because it is in transition, a combination of the familiar and the foreign, and also because the author will not let him die by his own hand.

But things must change in a story, the equilibrium must be broken, the protagonist must ride the wave of escalating tension to the top, over the top, in fact, to the other side where things will never be the same. This is what I will tell Tom Hanks: that as Martin stands at the back door he is on the literal threshold of change.

Tonight, he does not build a fire at the fence line, and so they come, droning like a distant biplane, tearing tomatoes from the vines, red innards coloring their mouths; they are hungry. Martin stands on the top stair, his right leg now growing numb beside his left, his hands cramping into claws. He smiles, descends, slumps toward them.

what it might feel like to hope

The mortician is a short man with sagging jowls and tufts of dark hair that curve over the tops of his ears, a man for whom phrases like *He's in a better place* and *The Lord giveth and the Lord taketh away* hold no sway or meaning. The mortician is a businessman; he neither contemplates nor cares whether the souls of the newly departed swirl through the ether toward a bright light where a final reckoning will be tallied by a saintly figure in flowing robes. The mortician cares about *life*, for he feels his primary duty is to the living, to demystify the event that often makes people feel guilty, makes them take responsibility—a little arrogantly, he thinks—for something entirely natural and inevitable despite their determination to convince themselves otherwise. The mortician offers to explain the death certificate in detail: You see here it says cardiac embolism, which is a runaway particle that obstructed the blood flow to his heart. *You didn't do that*, he wants to say, *his own body did that.*

The mortician is keenly aware of how a body can turn on a person without notice. Men keel over from heart attacks while delivering impassioned sermons from pulpits—the irony is not lost on the mortician, how these men died while thinking to save others—or while attempting to procreate, to immortalize themselves. And the women under them, the mortician thinks, must carry with them a sense of horror and satisfaction. If he could, the mortician would tell these women to be neither chastened nor proud, for they are merely witnesses to a body suddenly ending the long, arduous journey into nothingness. But it's not just the men; the mortician smooths and cuts into the sallow skin of women, some so small and frail the bones snap under his fingers, their hair thin and gauzy, follicles dead at the root. These bodies turn on the women not in a sudden, unpredictable rage but in a slow, methodical one, convincing them that they are not hungry so that the body can cannibalize itself, eat its own flesh until each cell loses its sense of purpose and succumbs to anarchy. The heart, liver, kidneys, they are smart: they know when to quit. But the lungs, stupid soldiers plodding stupidly toward their doom, insist on exhausting themselves, will continue to route oxygen to rogue cells, keeping the dead alive for days, even weeks. The mortician dismisses the Buddhist notion that each body contains a predetermined number of breaths, although it flutters through his mind like a small bird each time he cups a sharp jaw or touches the gnarled, ghostly hands. But he is a mortician, and so he puts his own hands to work, turning the head on its side and placing the fingers upright on the foam pad, dismissing the images of holocaust victims that anorexics generate even in businessmen.

The children: the mortician doesn't mind pumping their prostrate forms with fluid, folding their cold hands over their chests, pulling flowered anklets from their rigid feet. He makes them beautiful—well, beautiful enough—for their parents and aunts and grandparents. He makes them into something that is real enough for their families to say goodbye. Children's bodies, soft and weak, are often pushed past the boundaries of their ability to fight. *Anaphylactic shock, spinal meningitis, encephalitis—not your fault, not your fault, not your fault.*

The mortician listens to classical music, Tchaikovsky's "Nightingale" or Brahms's "Lullaby," when he embalms children. How do you perform your best work? The mortician is alone, and he is a businessman. So why does he listen to "The Little Russian" and "Snow Maiden" while tying silk ribbons and knotting small, striped ties? Perhaps the music underscores his sense of purpose while preoccupying his own heart. He listens to other things—opera usually—when he fashions the adults, or when he cooks homemade tortellini, or when he creaks into his stuffed chair to read Thomas Lemurra, his favorite author, one who refuses to allow any character to die.

Thomas Lemurra lives in Newport, in an inherited house with twenty-three cavernous rooms, many of them overlooking the Atlantic where it lashes the shore into a lazy U that forms a small cove beneath his master suite balcony. His wife, Alenz, has complained about the house—the ornate tapestries festooning the halls, the monogrammed silver, the sheer size for just the two of them. When he goes on book tours she pays the help to stay with her because she is frightened, for she knows the ghosts of her impoverished past in Mexico seek her, angry that she has not shared her good fortune, and that they will find her, like death finds the preacher and the lover, when she least expects it. Although there are twelve bedrooms in all, Alenz convinces Maria, or Luca, or the odd one who calls herself Ebony to sleep in her room on the wrought iron bed she has bought specifically for this purpose so that she will not face the demons alone. The bed is beautiful—burnished copper with crystal globes adorning each post, the iron fretwork welded into a fury of flowers and vines. But the bed has remained empty for months: Alenz has been ill and Lemurra has given up touring for the present. His wife has been plagued by violent, persistent fevers, immobilizing headaches and abdominal pains, yet doctors can find nothing physically wrong with her. Of course, she sends gold jewelry back to her family, even a small Picasso, the one Lemurra had presented to her three weeks after they'd met, for the city museum. But when she says *New church* or *Scholarship fund*, her husband touches her oblong face fondly. *Mi amor*, he says, *you are safe. You don't owe anyone anything.* But Lemurra is not a doctor; he is a novelist. He does not know how the body can suddenly turn on you. Perhaps if he had read the letters he'd received from the mortician more carefully, he would understand.

But Lemurra is too distracted to read anything from the letters but the things he most needs to read: how brilliantly he executes a phrase, how efficiently he compresses a life. What are the distractions of a wealthy, famous man? In the case of Thomas Lemurra, they are many: his wife's strange illness, his own recent forgetfulness, his fear that he will be unable to write another novel as good as his last. The praise he has basked in for the past two decades, he knows, will fade when his fans understand that he has spent the final coins of his creative fortune on the last book, luring characters to the brink of death in order to orchestrate their myriad salvations. How could he have known this tactic would mark him as the savior, would be the trademark of his work, would become the expectation of every reader who arrives at the tenth chapter desperate to be saved alongside the character with whom he now identifies? Would he have written his novels in this saved-from-the-brink-of-death format had he known he would feel forced—by the industry, by his fans, by himself!—to continue until he'd established a new genre, until he became the man to whom people looked for hope? What kind of writer would he have otherwise been? It's impossible to say, and his contemplations leave him resigned and weary. He thinks of the mortician then, when he is most hopeless, a rich man folding under the weight of regret, unable to even touch the specially molded ergonomic keyboard that was a gift from his publisher after *Lost and Found* hit the bestseller list. When he unfolds the mortician's letter, caressing it like a talisman, he denies the prescience of Bankcroft's request, for how could anyone know of his remorse? Still, there is comfort in these words that echo his own thoughts, that encourage him to do the thing he's always wanted to do:

Dear Mr. Lemurra,

It is a brilliant thing to create something out of nothing, masterfully and lovingly, to evoke life! But that, of course, is only half the story. I have hope, Mr. Lemurra, that you will do the sensible thing, that you will face the inevitable conclusion. What more can be done?

Sincerely, Thomas M. Bankcroft

Lemurra had noted when he retrieved the letter from a sack delivered that morning by his publisher the return address—a mortuary service; the lettering was a fine, understated calligraphy, and the envelope was textured, expensive. The mortician's note was atypical—not a religious fanatic praising him for seeing that life is eternal or a graduate student stunned by his inability to deconstruct the text—but short and sincere. Its arrival was timely, its impact strong; Lemurra began carrying the letter in his vest pocket, often stroking the soft linen paper as he sat on the hexagonal balcony watching waves gouge at the shore below. Perhaps he could write another novel for Bankcroft, for himself, though precisely how he would do this he could not tell. But maybe that was for the best: writers should not attempt to demystify the creative process, he thought. Don't think too much; just let it happen.

Actually, though, it has not happened for Lemurra in the year since his last book was published, although he often scratches furiously on any one of the twenty-three notebooks he has placed in each room of the house. Ideas, he says, for the next one. Alenz has read these ideas—boat sinks in shark-infested bay, shaman in modern America, Cubans attack Florida—but cannot see how they could ever arrange themselves into a novel. She is not a novelist, though, she is a woman running away from vengeful spirits, convinced that they will kill her for her selfishness, a woman who is slowly, unwittingly sacrificing her body to their will.

The mortician lives in a flat above his business in Wayland. He serves what an art council or a social worker might call the underserved, children with concave chests, women with tar-stained teeth, men carted from the automotive plant to the service entrance behind the building. Somebody loves them; somebody brings their Sunday best; somebody comes to caress the wayward strand of hair, to try to make them more beautiful than they ever really were. The mortician lets the living do what they will to survive this, the latest thing impossible to survive. Sometimes he smiles at their small ministrations, the light touch of rouge on the cheek, the cologne-dabbed comb pulled through the hair, smiles at the unnecessary tenderness, knowing this final interaction is likely the gentlest they've had with this person they love. He works diligently on the remains; he answers their questions; he touches a hand, a shoulder, but he knows his place. He is not the keeper of any special secret, for everyone knows where the winding path of life ends, but as a mortician he is, and must be, on speaking terms with death. *It's all right*, he wants to say, but he pulls back, contemplates the book he's currently reading, the opera in which he will later lose his thoughts.

Even Thomas Bankcroft sees himself as The Mortician, and this has nothing to do with the children soaping skeletons onto his street-side windows or the women lowering their eyes as he emerges into the parlor from the embalming room downstairs. The mortician inherited the business from his father, who also called himself The Mortician. They are not morbid people; they are business people. Under no circumstances does he wear his apron or gloves into the parlor, nor does he leave the door to the basement stairwell ajar. He does not engage in idle chatter with his customers, he does not charge more than ten percent over cost, and he does not exploit grief to sell mahogany coffins with pure silk lining.

After the funeral for a man who had dragged an oxygen canister around for two decades, after watching his daughters kiss his deeply etched face and clutch the casket bars as he was lowered into a muddy hole at Mount Olive Cemetery, after wondering how people are persistently dumbfounded by the inevitable, the mortician climbs the stairs to his flat and listens to Maria Callas sing arias about unrequited love and fallen heroes, and he is thankful that in his business he seldom encounters such things. He picks up Lemurra's *Lost and Found* just as Callas casts herself upon a golden dagger.

Alenz was a poor child who grew into a poor woman who delivered mild taquitos and iced beer to tourists at La Cantina in Acapulco. She did not mind the ersatz Mexican cuisine or the demanding patrons. On the contrary; she found that shy smiles and submissive glances often separated these gringos from their money, and she had three younger siblings and an aging father to consider. She did not mind, that is, until the day a drunken American stumbled into her, tipping an entire tray of gazpacho soup onto a group of retired tourists. "Dios mio," she cried, "disparatado hombre!" But as the man approached each diner, apologizing and offering to pay his laundering bill, Alenz softened.

"You are still crazy," she said to him, "but you are kind."

"Come away with me," he cried, and Alenz laughed because she'd heard stories about the hollow imagination and the irresponsible abandon of Americans, how they buy things they don't need and eat food they don't want simply because they can. She waved him away, forgot about him until, hours later when the tourists slid from barstools leaving behind slurred dreams and half-filled glasses, he emerged from the shadows and asked if she'd considered his offer. He was sober then, and wanted to tell her a story.

They sat on the restaurant's bamboo porch for a long while watching stars rearrange themselves into patterns neither could name, and then he began: "There was a man who had everything and had nothing, because to be without desire is to be dead. When he felt desire for the first time in many years—how many he could not tell since a man without desire is also a man for whom time is meaningless—he was grateful."

Alenz was not surprised by the story; in fact, she understood well the exaggeration and paradox that comprised the strange American's narrative, so in tune with the timbre of Mayan folklore that had wafted through the landscape of her childhood. Nor was she surprised when he rose and departed, silently, turned inward, curling himself around this newfound hope. She fell in love with him that night under a cryptic sky and married him three weeks later, this strange storyteller with his books and his offerings of flowers and words and a small, color-stained Picasso. Her initial joy had precluded her from understanding that she had left behind more than her town, her home, her father: she had left behind the responsibilities that had forged her, had imprinted upon her a purpose, had assured her that she had, each day, earned her God-given life.

Now Alenz, lying in bed with sweat-soaked towels across her brow, her heart thrumming to the death drums echoing from two thousand miles away, blames not her husband, who has been generous, after all, but herself, for not learning the lesson of every childhood story and every ancient myth: that money cannot save you, that happiness is not free, that one who denies her calling will not be spared.

The mortician is heartened when by chapter 11 of *Lost and Found* the abducted victim has not been found, has, in fact, been given up for dead by all but her grieving parents, whose days consist of prayers and pills. He is not upset—there is nothing death can say to the mortician that will surprise him, no form it can take that will shake him—but he sees Lemurra's slow reaching toward the truth in this suspense of assurance, in this life held in abeyance. Yet it seems certain that the girl will survive—the title is proof enough—certain that Lemurra will not disappoint his disciples, and this disappoints the mortician, who holds forth a distant hope that Lemurra is stumbling toward a fuller reality. Others have done it, written about death, callously and superficially, he thinks. But Lemurra, a man who has made the conscious decision to outwit death, is surely more qualified by this very avoidance to confront it. Hasn't he poised one hero on the banks of the river Lethe, another in the arms of the Medusa? Certainly he considered all possible fates of the character on the flaming dirigible, the one in the ambulance, the one on the bridge. Who better to accost death than the man who has spent years across the chessboard from it, scheming against, running from and outmaneuvering it? What he won't acknowledge, however, is that his efforts are in vain. Death is simply there, endlessly patient, waiting for the novelist to run out of moves.

The mortician closes his eyes then, mouths the words as Licia Albanese sings of living for the moment in *Manon*. *If you can only do that, Mr. Lemurra*, he thinks, *you will understand that the moment contains all, even death*. But people do not want to stare into the face of truth—Lemurra's literary fame is proof of that—and even though Manon sings of living for the moment, tempting eternity with wild abandon, he wonders if she would sing as sweetly if she knew she'd be dead before the next act. The mortician wedges the parchment bookmark carefully between pages 310 and 311 and with his slippered foot gently slides the novel under his chair. He will write to Lemurra while life hangs in the balance, while hope in the liberating acceptance of death flutters in his chest, before the unrealistic ending colors his thoughts:

> Dear Mr. Lemurra,
>
> You have renewed my hope that you will carry the literate nation into the farthest realms of truth in ways both chilling and sublime. No one else, I'm afraid, is qualified. You have their attention, Mr. Lemurra, and now you must tell them the truth, you must allow life to proceed on its natural course. Ferry us from delusion and denial into a reality we can embrace, one that will open the doors to a fuller appreciation of life! I have the utmost confidence that you can, Mr. Lemurra. I have the utmost confidence that you will.
>
> Yours in admiration, Thomas M. Bankcroft

Lemurra sits on the balcony staring into the sky, his head throbbing, a bottle of vodka gripped in one hand and Bankcroft's most recent letter dangling from the other. He's not taken calls in days, even from his agent, whom he'd considered a good friend until his creative well ran dry. He's hired live-in nurses, paid specialists in bacterial infections and digestive tract diseases to see his wife, and other than dehydration they are unable to diagnose anything. All that is left is to wire a $70,000 check for the Alenz

Lemurra wing of the Manuel de Navarrette Library, to underwrite the final restoration phase of the Orozco Cathedral, to sponsor a reading program for all Zamoran public schools. And so he does, but when he tells his wife that he has offered up his gifts, has placated the vengeful spirits, she simply stares at him, as if from under deep water.

Now, as he cowers under a moonless sky downing large amounts of liquor on an empty stomach, he holds his aching head in his hands and considers Bankcroft's letter, one by which he is both confused and enlightened. Does Bankcroft know that he is confronting death even as he reads the words that would otherwise confound him? The world is imbued with mystery, he thinks, and he is a desperate man; will giving death its due in print placate it, direct it away from his wife, who writhes in her bed and calls out to the Virgin for relief? Of course not, Lemurra thinks, how could it? But Lemurra has already done things even more illogical to save his wife, and so he considers whether he can kill a character sympathetically, believably. He does not care what the New York book reviewers will think, does not care if his publisher deserts him, does not care if he disappoints his fans. He only cares if it will work, and he contemplates the curious chain of events that brought him to this hollow logic. When he stumbles to his oak-paneled office and falls into the thickly-padded leather chair, he tries to imagine what he'll write, but his hands tremble, hovering over the keyboard as if casting a spell. When he envisions death—the blue tint of the corpse from lead poisoning, the bloated body of the drowning victim, the skeleton scorched by napalm burns—it feels unreal, almost comical. He imagines the characters who have inhabited his former novels in the precarious situations into which he originally placed them now experiencing wholly different outcomes; the elderly man will not be pulled from the waves, the military plane will be detected on enemy radar, the abducted girl's body will be found in the cabin from which, in *Lost and Found*, she currently stumbles. But it doesn't work, and he realizes that the only death he can imagine with utter clarity is the death of his wife. He will call the mortician, he decides, for whom better to explain death in its graphic finality, whom better to help him summon a specter vivid enough to fool the gods?

Thomas Bankcroft lifts his eyes from page 323, imagines Don Giovanni being dragged to his death by a statue, Faust giving his soul to the devil on a snow-covered street in Wittenberg, Aida buried alive in an Egyptian crypt. None of that will do, of course, because death is not so mythical, not so absurd. Death comes expectedly, even for opera characters, whose authors plot their doom long before they put pen to paper or sound that first ominous note. He rises, places a scratched recording of *Carmen* on the turntable, soon loses himself in the voice of Mirella Freni, who sings brightly, cheerfully, for she does not see the knife in José's hand.

Bankcroft is summoned from his reverie by the jangle of his telephone, which at first seems to come from within his own mind, so caught up in the contemplation of death is he. He answers, and initially thinks the call is a joke, that someone is imitating the famous author, though he cannot fathom who would have the knowledge of his admiration to orchestrate the prank. But he then hears the desperation he knows so well, the gasp and stutter of a person in the throes of loss, and he soon understands that death now courts Lemurra's wife. While previously prepared to convince the man that death should be summoned up in print, displayed bold before the literate world, Bankcroft is stunned into silence when Lemurra makes his request.

"So you think she will live?" he finally asks. "If you write this?"

"It's the only thing I can do. Please come, Mr. Bankcroft," he urges, "with your books and your stories and your visions of death."

Though he has not traveled in years and will have to close his business for several days, he will go. Maybe his plane will crash, he thinks, maybe Lemurra will write about death. Maybe his wife will live.

So he will be here in three days, Lemurra thinks with relief as he trades the bottle for the keyboard, downs seven Ibuprofen tablets to relieve the wracking pain in his skull. He dusts the office, tests the tape recorder, clears his desk. He types up questions for the mortician, abstract at first: What does death look like? Feel like? How is it to be alone with the dead? Then pointed and precise: What happens to the body during suffocation? Who decides if the casket will be opened or closed?

He goes to his wife, tells her that Bankcroft is coming, that together they will write her back to life, and she smiles the delusional smile of the fevered. He speaks in riddles, it seems, assures her in whispers that he has found a way to save her; she envisions her village floating weightlessly over the ocean, the people dancing in robes of light, pulling her up, up, up into their shiny arms.

Before he can depart, Bankcroft must prepare the body of an elderly woman who had died while eating a slab of ribs, a longtime friend of his father whose will specified that Bankcroft's services be procured. Even as he grows angry with himself for proceeding in a distracted state, he continues to ponder what he will say to Lemurra, understands for the first time the gross inadequacy of language, admires anew the author's ability to conjure and sustain life with nothing more than words. But he has not Lemurra's literary talent; surely his wife's passing will reveal to the author more succinctly than any letter he could write the power and certainty of death. He will be left not to convince but to comfort, for he finally sees the irony in his undertaking and realizes what a fool he's been: language cannot convince people to embrace death any more than it can save Alenz Lemurra's life. For two days Bankcroft shambles around his house, practicing speeches that feel wooden, deciding ultimately that he will lend words to his thoughts spontaneously. Both eager and anxious about seeing Lemurra, he packs his clothes into a leather valise and arrives at the airport three hours early on the day of his departure. Maybe Alenz has already died, he thinks. His connecting flight from Chicago to Newport is delayed, so he sits in the molded plastic chair, contemplating. Perhaps he should maintain the role of objective expert, simply supplying verisimilitude to an author whose fervent wish is to trade one life for another. Bankcroft accepted the invitation easily, and now the uncertainty of his venture weighs on him like a sodden overcoat.

The taxi drops him in front of a towering mansion, but his judgments are tempered by sympathy. We are all equal, he thinks, we are all the same in death. A stern-looking man dressed in black opens the door after Bankcroft knocks, and Bankcroft sees that the man is bent by grief. This is not Lemurra, the handsome author, but a butler or a valet, someone with the air of rigid competency.

"My plane," he apologizes. "I'm sorry."

"Come in. Please."

"I am too late," he says.

"Yes," the man nods. "There is nothing you could have done."

"I'm Thomas Bankcroft—"

"Yes. The letters. We found them this morning."

Ah, an attorney, he thinks, someone who clearly had little faith in Lemurra's plan.

"May I see him?"

The man seems startled by his request, and Bankcroft quickly rescinds. "I'm sorry. This is a bad time, certainly."

"There is no good time, Mr. Bankcroft. This way."

They drift across a great hall toward what appears to be another wing of the house, and the man slows considerably when he approaches a set of intricately carved doors, perhaps fearful of causing an unwelcome interruption.

"I'm sure he would have wanted *your* services," he says.

Bankcroft shakes his head weakly. "No, of course, I—"

For the first time in many years Bankcroft is at a loss for words in the face of death, tries to collect his thoughts and form them into a speech of heartfelt comfort. But he remains silent when the man turns the brass handles on the double doors and he glimpses the casket at the far end of the room. The condolences he's offered clients in the past now feel empty to him, and he is suddenly relieved that a cursory search of the room does not reveal Lemurra slumped in a chair, disconsolate, staring vacantly through a rain-fogged window.

"He would have it this way," the man says, nodding. "The publicity."

"I understand," Bankcroft says, although he doesn't. How can someone—anyone—conduct a home viewing? It's no longer done. He realizes suddenly that we are not equal, even in death, and it is then, as he approaches the casket, that he sees the body inside is Lemurra's.

"My God," he says, feeling an unfamiliar weakness in his legs, "what's this?"

The man takes his arm, guides him toward a chair. "Please sit down, Mr. Bankcroft."

Bankcroft sloughs off his concern, struggles toward comprehension. "He said his wife was ill. I thought—"

"I was ill, Mr. Bankcroft."

Bankcroft turns to see a small woman standing under the arched doorway, her face a dark mask. She stares at him sternly as she moves toward him, then softens when she sees his expression. "I'm sorry. I thought you knew. The news. My husband's death—it was sudden, but it was on the news. An aneurysm, Mr. Bankcroft. I'm Alenz Lemurra."

Bankcroft's thoughts—the unfairness, the unfinished work, even his own complicity in willing death to Lemurra's doorstep—are ridiculous and selfish to him, and so he remains silent, stares at the sleeve of Alenz's black dress.

"He was quite ill," she says as she sits beside him. He suddenly sees the irony, the man who outwits death is dead, the man who would trade one life for another now has. "We didn't know. The aneurysm. All the medical staff here and we didn't know."

Bankcroft sits quietly until his shock collapses into sadness. As the black sleeve at which he stares blurs before him, he hears the music stop and the singers lose their voices, sees the columns and statues of the opera set crash to the stage below. But this is false, he thinks, an imitation of tragedy he's conjured out of desperation to avoid the real one, the only man who'd ever offered real hope now gone. His thoughts circle to his clients and he contemplates the many ways he's failed them, dismissing their responses to death as naïve and unnecessary. Their small acts, he now understands, were attempts to restore a semblance of order, to exact some control over a life suddenly tipped off its axis. Who was he to deny them that, even subtly? Each breath catches in his throat as the voices scream through his mind: Rigoletto begging his daughter not to die, Cio-Cio crying as she falls dead before the Buddha, Aida wailing from the crypt.

"No," he whispers to stop the mad singing, and he rises and moves toward Lemurra. The casket handles are brushed silver, the wood stained deep red, and the bright white lining shimmers like an opulent nest. Bankcroft berates himself for his inability to confront death now, for losing himself in details, his long-term hypocrisy now birthing a desire for self-punishment. In a sudden motion he looks to Lemurra's face, a pallid face, and stops himself from hiding behind a critique of the mortician's skills. What does it matter?

Putting his hand to his own face, he catches the tears that death has pulled from him, but they continue to come and he lets them. He touches Lemurra's cold hand with his own, and he suddenly wishes for something more. As quickly as he quells this foolish, irrational desire it is replaced by a thought that he allows to unfold. He wonders if someone awaits the author at the end of his present journey. Bankcroft then wishes, selfishly, that Lemurra had saved just enough breaths to teach him what it might feel like to hope.

little birds

May told Dina to take the chair or she'd regret it for the rest of her life.

"I don't want it," said Dina.

"Take the goddamn chair."

Dina stared at her mother, mute.

"If I weren't so tired, I'd cry," said May.

"I'm not taking it."

"Anything to embarrass me, to make me look bad to the family."

"Like you need me for that."

May stared back. "I could kill you right now."

"I thought you were tired."

"I could rest afterward."

The mahogany chair was armless and quite small. In a large house it would look like a piece of children's furniture, and Dina figured that that was why her mother didn't want it. This was simply May's combined attempt to control her while casting an insult at her tiny condo and its minimalist décor. Why else would she be so adamant about a stupid piece of furniture? Dina thought that the chair might actually look large in her minuscule living room but couldn't imagine the burnt sienna brocade against her lavender wall. She told her mother repeatedly that she didn't want the chair until May finally asked what she would like instead.

"Her knitting needles," said Dina. "I want Grandma's knitting needles."

There was a lengthy pause before May said, "What are you, wacky?"

"You asked me."

"You don't know how to knit."

"I can learn."

"Okay," said May. "Maybe you can knit yourself a chair."

Rhona, May's mother and Dina's grandmother, had died three weeks earlier while gumming a slab of ribs. Angry at having to pound on the oak door for several minutes before extracting the house key from her Gucci clutch, May was stunned when she stormed into the kitchen to find her mother sleeping on the table, her fist wrapped tightly around a short end.

"You know you're not supposed to eat ribs," May scolded while trying to make out the strange pink blob in the glass near her mother's right hand. "Mother?"

Even after May shook Rhona several times with no response, she continued to think CPR, 911, heart attack, indigestion. She didn't think death until one of the paramedics, apparently concerned about staining the sheets on the gurney, started wiping sauce from Rhona's fingers instead of administering mouth-to-mouth.

"Well," said May, who in a certain state of shock dismissed the paramedic as one would a carpet cleaner, "that will be all then."

She called Dina immediately from her cell phone because, in her distraction, she somehow believed that her mother's landline, like her mother, no longer worked.

"Your grandmother's dead," she announced.

"Oh, my God!"

"I need you to come over here. I can't remember how to drive."

"Yes," said Dina, muffling sobs. "How did she die?"

"The ribs," said May. "It must have been the ribs."

"I'm coming."

May sat at what she mentally labeled the Last Supper table and realized, on closer inspection, that the strange substance in the glass flanking Rhona's right hand was her dental plate.

May began her assault concerning the chair almost immediately. During the funeral service, she leaned toward Dina and said, "It would look marvelous in your foyer."

Dina dismissed her mother's behavior in church as grief-triggered delirium. "We'll talk later," she said.

"Later it may be gone," said May. "Let's pick it up after the funeral. Before Lena and Gretchen get it."

"I don't want it."

"Yes, you do."

"Let Aunt Lena have it—"

"Over my dead body—"

"Mother!"

"I don't want her to have it."

"Then why don't you take it?"

"Me?" she asked, fingers fanned across her chest. "Well, *I* don't want it."

The evening of the funeral, May fell into a deep reverie about the chair. She remembered Miguel striking the heavy wooden legs with a chisel, his back muscles flexing, how she stopped herself from touching his wet hair. Even now she can see the chair's skeleton, a mere frame of unfinished wood, and she could smell the sawdust on his lips. She was nineteen.

May had helped him choose a floral pattern for the back and seat cushions, one she was certain her mother would love, and he finished the work that very day. He said he could wait no longer before presenting it to her parents.

"Here," he said without preliminaries. "I love May and I'm going to marry her."

Dina was late for their weekly lunch date, and May waited impatiently for her daughter at her favorite restaurant, The Precinct.

"Well," said May as Dina slid into the red velvet chair opposite her, "maybe we should give you Mother's clock, too."

"Did you bring the needles?"

"No. I thought we could pick them up after lunch. I thought you might want to see the house again before it's sold."

Dina was glad May had thought of this but didn't say so. "Okay."

"Excuse me," May said to a passing waiter with gold epaulettes on his shoulders. "Can we have some water?"

The man looked disgusted. "I am a lieutenant," he said. "Detective!" he snapped at a teenage boy with a bad haircut and a crystal water pitcher. "Here." He glanced down his nose at May and Dina's table.

The detective, who wore only a badge on his shirt pocket, poured the water with resignation.

"It's too bad you didn't detect that we needed water," said May. "You'll never make lieutenant that way."

"Sorry, Ma'am."

"Never mind," said May while slipping a five-dollar bill over the badge and into the boy's pocket as Dina slumped behind the large flaps of her menu.

"Thank you," said the boy, bowing slightly before rushing off to the kitchen.

"Why can't we go to normal places for lunch?" asked Dina, who had never understood the heady power her mother derived from verbally bludgeoning wait staff.

"What's wrong with this place?"

Dina surveyed the room and grimaced.

May sighed. "It's your generation," she said as she perused her menu absently, "you have no respect for the police."

Despite Dina's objections, they drove in the same car to Rhona's house after lunch. The house was an old colonial, built in 1937 by the grandson of a lumber baron for his new wife, a demanding and paranoid socialite who personally directed construction of its custom features: hideaway cabinets for her jewelry, soundproof bedroom walls in the event that they had children, and a revolving panel that hid the entrance to an underground tunnel leading to what then was a horse stable. Rhona was charmed by the house and bought it shortly after the death of her second husband. She allowed her grandchildren to play in her soundproof bedroom and, much to the horror of their parents, encouraged them to scamper through the dirt-floored tunnel beneath the house.

"I've raised a bunch of snobs," she'd once said, staring at her three daughters. "I'll do a better job with my grandchildren."

"But, Mother—" said Gretchen.

"Are you worried they'll get mud on their Birkenstocks? Tear their Hilfiger jeans? I'll replace them."

Although Rhona never said as much, her daughters felt she was overcompensating for her grandchildren's absentee fathers, who were more often than not away at medical conventions in California, shareholder meetings in New York, corporate mergers in Tokyo.

So, the children played tag or tug-of-war in the narrow tunnel with flashlights. When they tired of that, they emerged like groundhogs through a wooden door that had been cut into the floor of the stable. Rhona had converted the stable into a large gardening shed where the children spent hours playing with her sun bonnets and weeding gloves, where they gave one another wheelbarrow rides at breakneck speeds around the building's perimeter. It was always Rhona who walked the eighth-mile to the building to retrieve her five grandchildren for supper, and they sang and danced across the manicured lawn to the house where her daughters would immediately demand that their children wash before supper.

Dina thought about her grandmother's voice, the tunnel and the stable as May maneuvered her Town Car through the narrow streets of the old subdivision, lush with cherry blossom trees and lilac bushes. She recalled the white shawl her grandmother had knitted for her First Communion when she was seven, how it was silk-lined and how each flower had a shiny sequin in its center.

"It's beautiful, Momma," she had said. "It sparkles."

May thanked Rhona for the shawl and promptly placed it back in the box. Dina never wore the shawl because May had said that it was too small. It wasn't until much later—after homemade afghans, sweaters and scarves had been permanently swallowed up by closets and when, as an adult, Dina looked at her communion pictures—that she realized the truth. Dina, like the other second-grade girls, wore an ankle-grazing white lace dress with a tailored jacket and gloves with mother-of-pearl buttons.

When May paused on the front porch of her mother's house, took a deep breath, turned to Dina and demanded she open the door, Dina snatched the key from her mother's trembling hand, disgusted by her melodrama. She pushed open the heavy door and a small square of yellow paper fluttered onto the foyer's ceramic tile floor.

"What's this?" she asked, stooping to pick it up.

Printed in bold black letters on the Post-It note was the word *Gretchen.*

"It must have fallen off," said May, staring at a large gilt-framed mirror on the wall.

Dina glanced around the room and saw a sea of yellow notes clinging haphazardly to lamps, pictures, furniture, even curtains.

"It was the easiest way," May sighed. "For the movers."

Dina entered the living room slowly, stepping around a note fixed to the Persian carpet that read *May*. She focused on the notes, the edges curled into wings that she expected would begin to move, slowly at first and then with a speed that would lift furniture off the floor and saucers off the table where they would hang suspended in the air waiting for her to join them when the carpet on which she stood took flight.

"They didn't want it," said May, staring at the hand-woven rug. "What was I supposed to do?"

"Didn't she have a will?"

"Yes. It said we should work it out amongst ourselves."

Dina plopped onto the thick carpet and laughed. Then she saw the chair. The ceramic doll her grandmother had placed on it was gone, and a Post-It note on its back fluttered in the small breeze sent from the vent below. It wasn't until she crawled over that she saw the word *Dina* scrawled on the paper.

"I've already told Lena and Gretchen you want it," said May.

"Why?"

"Because you do. You just don't know you do."

"Where are the needles?"

"I'll just look foolish if you don't take the chair now."

"I'm sure it will be nothing new to them."

"Won't you do this for me?"

"No," said Dina. "No, I won't."

Dina walked through the house while May pawed through her mother's knitting basket for the needles. None of the other notes had her name on them, and for this she was thankful. She climbed the creaky stairs to her grandmother's bedroom, closed the door behind her and peeled a yellow note from the oak headboard. She crumpled it up and placed it in her pocket, then threw herself on the bed, buried her face in the knit bedspread and cried.

"What am I supposed to do now?" she screamed into the pillow. "I can't deal with her alone!"

She slid off the bed and stared at herself in the mirror above her grandmother's dressing table. "Coward," she accused her reflection, wiping her eyes with the sleeve of her jacket. Rhona stared at her from a photograph below, smiling, comforting, and Dina smiled back. "You're terrific," she said, "putting a picture of yourself in your own bedroom." She took the photo out of the frame, slid it into her pocket and placed the frame back on the table. She then walked the lengthy second-floor hall, but the sight of the winged notes kept her from entering the rooms.

The chandelier above her clanked in the breeze from the balcony window, and Dina looked up to see the word *Lena* staring at her from one of its crystal arms. "Little birds," she whispered. "Little vultures."

May was waiting for Dina at the bottom of the stairs. "Here," she said, shoving the knitting basket at her, "take the whole goddamn thing."

Dina wrapped both arms around the basket and headed toward the front door, but May had moved in the opposite direction, and when Dina turned she saw that her mother was sitting on the chair, stroking the seat cushion.

"I can't keep it," she said, turning to Dina.

"C'mon, Mom."

"The movers are coming tomorrow," said May. "Will you be home when they deliver it?"

Before Rhona could thank Miguel for the chair her husband interrupted. "Mr. Sanchez—"

"Miguel."

"Miguel, you're a furniture maker?" he asked with polite condescension.

"And a good one, sir."

"How much money does a furniture maker *make*?"

Rhona shot her husband an angry look. Miguel was one of the twin sons of their beloved maid, Carmen, whom she had hired years ago after she'd left her alcoholic husband.

"Don't answer that," he said, suddenly annoyed. "You can't marry my daughter." He turned to May and simply said, "Someday you'll thank me for this" before marching from the room.

May turned to Rhona. "Why don't you do something?" she cried.

Rhona stared at the carpet, shook her head and sighed. Because Miguel was there, she did not say what she wished to, what they all knew: that May could never survive on love alone, that she had become a slave to money sometime between the porcelain dolls and the designer ball gowns. That she requested her father's permission was evidence enough that she wouldn't marry without the security of his money.

"Why don't *you* do something?" said Rhona.

Because Rhona loved the fine craftsmanship and lustrous fabric of the chair, it remained in the parlor for years, serving first as a trigger of fiery resentment in May and later as a reminder to her of her weakness and her mother's disappointment in her. She saw the irony as the chair resumed its role as a symbol of estrangement between a mother and daughter, but she felt powerless to stop it.

Dina liked her empty foyer, the sound of her voice echoing through her small home, something returning to her. The chair did not belong here, was just another of May's attempts to control her, attempts that had grown more desperate since she refused to move into the large townhouse in an affluent subdivision that May had bought and decorated for her. She was tired and a headache loomed behind her eyes when she arrived home from her grandmother's house. She slipped off her jacket and tossed it onto the floor, then reached into the pocket of her jeans and extracted her grandmother's photo and a crumpled yellow note that read *May*. Stuck to the back of the paper was the key she had taken from her mother's hand earlier and had forgotten to return. It felt cold and large, its shadow playing across her bare walls when she held it before a floor lamp.

Dina slipped the key back into her pocket then drove her Volkswagen through the silent streets to her grandmother's house. The living room was in motion, flowing under waves of yellow notes until she snapped on a torchiere lamp. The light lent definition to the notes, and for a moment it seemed as if her grandmother's things were flaking apart, disintegrating. She started downstairs with the mirror and the carpet and moved through the house until each note had been replaced by one with a different name. The Post-It on the back of the chair continued to flutter in the vent breeze until Dina replaced it with the crumpled note from her pocket. Her headache was gone when she sank onto the chair and realized for the first time just how uncomfortable it was.

a short distance behind us

Braelynn and I have been operating at the intersection of *I Love You* and *Fuck Off* for the past year, fighting and forgiving at breakneck speeds. We're both tired, but apparently not too tired to crawl into a cramped economy car and head west together. We are determined to work things out, to change our context, to see each other from a new angle.

The car is loaded–luggage, water, snacks–and we're eager to put some miles behind us, both literally and figuratively. So what if I studied the map and plotted the route, shopped for the food and packed the tent, topped off the gas tank and checked the weather; I don't mind, really. But is it so hard for Brae to order the small instead of the grande latte at Starbucks before we hit the road? We're barely past the Illinois state line before she's telling me to stop, that she has to piss, that if I don't pull over she's going to throw herself out of the car. This doesn't sound like a bad idea, but on second thought I realize that her plan is fraught with complications, so I swerve into the first gas station I see and slam on the brakes, imagining the liquid in her bladder sloshing. She shoots me the stink eye and I know she knows what I'm thinking every time all of the time, that if she had wet her pants right there on the front seat of the rented Jetta I would have only pretended to be sorry. When she goes inside and approaches the counter I imagine she's telling the clerk that I kidnapped her, to call the police, to hide her in the back among the cases of potato chips and warm beer until they arrive.

She takes her time, no doubt about that, and I clutch the map my father demanded I take, scanning the route I'd highlighted in yellow marker, a pretty straight line from Chicago to California, though for the first time I realize just how long that line is. The sun is baking the windshield and I remind myself that for the next two weeks my father can't bark orders at me from under his dented hard hat, eyes squinting disapproval as I stare at him, trowel in hand, that for the next fourteen days I won't have to navigate the hidden shoals of his erratic temper, so I start feeling better. In the time it takes Brae to empty her bladder I also think about why we're taking this trip, how we agreed the night before *not* to allow the small things that typically ruin our efforts ruin our efforts this time. Does she bring a coffee for me, the man who's been driving for two hours, the one who stayed up until midnight checking tires and filling ice cube trays while she slept the sleep of the dead? A little consideration, that's all I'm saying.

THE NEXT ONE HUNDRED MILES are a pastiche of feet thumping and Bjork's tortured screams echoing from the speakers, and I have to wonder what I'm doing with this woman. Who listens to Bjork? When I stop to use the bathroom at a Clark station she pitches a fit about how we're losing time but beats me to the attendant for the restroom key.

"Want me to drive for a while?" she asks as I exit the station.

My first reaction is to say no, but this is a long trip and Brae tends to do all right on the straightaways. Put her in traffic and you have a real problem. I'm not insulting women drivers—my mother has always been a skillful and conscientious driver—but Braelynn has totaled two cars in the last four years. When we first met she told me she had broken her arm in a Go-Kart accident and I said, "Based on how you drive your car I'm not surprised." She laughed. In those days I could say things like that. In those playful days we would share food and secrets, scream the lyrics of Beatles' songs in the car, pretend we were matadors and FBI agents. "Drs. Manny and Blanche Liebowitz," I would announce to restaurant hosts, who sometimes ushered us to a secluded table in the back and recommended meals that were not on the menu. Once we convinced a waitress that we were dancers with the touring Bolshoi Ballet–we were both young and lithe, Brae with her large eyes and hollowed cheekbones and me with my dimpled chin and bulky arms, and even though our Russian accents were appalling, she asked for our autographs. I signed as Anton Chekhov and she was Anna Karenina.

When I plop down into the passenger seat and eject the CD, Brae smiles sweetly and doesn't even mount an argument when I swap Bjork for Miles Davis. Why would she? Because even though the agreement is passenger picks music, she always argues. I return the smile before she starts the car and promptly backs into a man who had wanted nothing more than to pay for his gas and drive to the senior center where he plays checkers every Friday afternoon. The man is slumped over the trunk of the Jetta as if he's hugging it, trying to keep it from driving away, and I tear out of the car and pull him up, gently, as Brae stands there, horrified, hands over her mouth as if waiting to capture the scream that is plotting its escape.

"Call an ambulance," I shout, but she remains a statue.

The old guy rights himself, throws off my arm and starts hobbling toward the station, and I follow him, ask if he's all right, if I should call the police. He says hell no, it was just a bump, he's not going to any hospital where they'd kill him for sure. As the man shambles down the snack aisle, the clerk tells me the old guy doesn't have a valid driver's license, that he meets his friends every week at the Rockville Senior Center to play board games. "You just knocked him a little sideways," he says. "Big deal." Brae comes in, her face pale, looking nervous, upset, ready to fall apart. She yells at the poor guy, "Why'd you walk behind my car?" He looks at her as if she's just spoken in Swahili, then wobbles toward the counter, where he and the clerk carry on a conversation as if we're not even there. I tell Brae to be quiet, to get back in the car, to give me the keys. She exits the gas station, marches toward the Jetta and promptly vomits across the passenger side door.

When I reach her she is bent over, holding her stomach and heaving.

"Are you all right?" I ask as I pull her hair from her face and she nods but there are tears in her eyes.

"I was distracted," she says. "I'm sorry, Jake."

"Me too," I say, and I am. I help her into the passenger seat, buckle her in and do my best to squeegee the remains of her breakfast off the side-view mirror.

As we drive to the Tim Horton's next door so she can clean up, I tell her that it's all right, that the old man is a real firecracker, that it'll take a lot more than a three-thousand-pound car to sideline him, that she can take a nap while I drive the next leg of the trip. When she comes out of the restaurant she looks a lot better, and I don't say anything when she places the large steaming cup of coffee into a rubber nook in the console. Before she even takes a sip, she's snoring.

The only voice I hear for the next several hours is that of Etta James, and I let the silken sounds of the sax and the low grumble of James's throaty warble wrap me in the kind of soft peace I've not felt in months, lull me into a stupor that almost ends with the front end of the car jammed into a metal guardrail. I swerve just in time, and Brae's head pops up from the headrest, her eyes filled with both sleep and horror.

"A prairie dog," I say.

"What?"

"Or a squirrel."

"I should drive," she says.

I bite my tongue and say, "Let's stop for dinner. If you feel up to it."

"Sure," she says as she caresses her belly. "I'm starving." Then she lifts the coffee cup from its holder and tests its heft. "Why didn't you drink it?" she asks.

"That was mine?"

"Hazelnut cappuccino," she says. "Couldn't you smell it? I thought I was going to vomit all over again."

THE DINER IN OMAHA IS all red vinyl and chrome, Elvis photos and grease, waitresses with coin dispensers slung across their hips. "I bet our waitress will be named Rosie," I say and Brae squints at me.

"Why would she be named Rosie?"

"Because of this." I swivel my head around the restaurant. "You know, it's a cliché."

"You're a cliché," she snaps.

"That doesn't even make sense."

"I'm just hungry," she says, running her fingers through her rumpled hair. "You know I get cranky when I'm hungry."

"Well, you must always be hungry."

I laugh, because this is one of those things we used to joke about, but she is already sliding from the booth, and I wonder if she's heading toward the restroom or the parking lot. That's why I keep the car keys. Brae has left me at worse places than this: Wrigley Field, a Barenaked Ladies concert, my Aunt Pem's sixtieth birthday party staring at shelves of Precious Moments figurines until my cab arrived, my aunt wringing her hands, sweat soaking the armpits of her flowered housedress. Why did she leave me there? I don't even remember.

She returns just as Harriet, a waitress so old she looks petrified, shuffles up to our table and slurs something unintelligible.

I smile broadly and say, "This is my wife, Blanche, and I am Dr. Liebowitz."

"Come again?" Harriet leans toward me.

I point to Brae. "This is Blanche and I am Dr. Manny Liebowitz. Pleased to meet you."

Harriet shakes her head and fiddles with a dial on her hearing aid, and Brae looks mortified before yelling, "I'll have the burger special, medium well, pickle on the side. And an iced tea."

Harriet nods, though she's written nothing on her order pad, before turning her wrinkled eye on me.

"Do you have veggie burgers?" I shout and Brae's eyes widen; one of our pastimes is tallying the number of cows I've personally consumed over the carnivorous course of my life.

"Sure," huffs the fossilized waitress. "This isn't the *fifties.*"

I make a show of looking around and taking in the restaurant's time-stamped paraphernalia before yelling, "I beg to differ."

Harriet stares at me, and then she and Brae exchange that look, the look of the beleaguered yet patient woman.

"He'll also have the special," shouts Brae, "and an ice water."

"Actually," I say, "I'd like two chili dogs and a large Coke."

Harriet brings two specials and we eat in silence.

In all fairness, Brae isn't usually this mean; she's just mad at me. I met her five years ago when I broke my collarbone during a friendly football game and she was the ER nurse who prepped me for X-rays. I don't know if it was Demerol or testosterone, but when she leaned over to place the lead apron over my chest, brushing my arm with her left breast and smelling like hazelnut cappuccino, I asked her to marry me. Now she wants to take me up on it. Sure, I'm balking. She says that we're getting old, that we've been dating for too long, that it's time to have kids. I say that twenty-nine is not old, that we'll be together forever, that children will destroy us. Brae says I'm immature; I say we're not ready. I love her, but I don't love being treated like a child, I don't love Bjork and the Beastie Boys, I don't love being left at Aunt Pem's double-wide. Who's the immature one here?

We pull into a KOA campground in Wyoming before dark and grab a site on a small lake. After pitching the tent, I load briquettes into the grill, douse them with lighter fluid and watch them ignite.

"You're a pyro, you know that," says Brae as she approaches with the cooler.

"I am Captain Inferno!" I shout.

"Here," she says, "help me with this."

We grill steaks and corn on the cob and eat at a splintered picnic table.

"This is good," says Brae, who eats ravenously and without shame, butter coating her fingers and chin.

She is a good camper, which is why I brought the tent, convinced her to forego the cheap motels with mildewed bedspreads and rusted swimming pools. Our song is in tune out here, the division of duties fair and satisfying, the camaraderie high: it's us against the world, or it's just us, really. Why can't it be this simple back home? The campfire is blazing by the time she clears the picnic table, and we sit together staring at the flickering lights sprouting from the orange wood beneath.

I stare into the sky searching for constellations, though since we're unable to identify them we've simply made up names that fit the shapes. "There's Tilted Lampshade, Pencil Sharpener, Colossal Mouse."

Brae looks up and squints.

"Is that Broken Fan?" she asks.

"Yup."

"Then that must be Mim's Hat?"

"Yep, and Sherlock's Pipe above that."

"Kids would like this," she says. "A kid would think this is cool."

My stomach tightens and I quell the small revolution growing there. "You mean camping? Star naming?"

"Well, yeah, all of it." She looks at me for a few seconds and then turns back to the sky. We listen to the fire crackle, fall into a relaxed silence.

"Yesterday," I sing softly, "all our troubles seemed so far away—"

"What's that supposed to mean?" she snaps.

"Nothing. Why does *everything* have to mean *something*?"

"Because everything does."

"I thought that was your favorite Beatles song."

"Not right now."

"Well, what would you like to hear? Bjork? Siouxsie and the Banshees? Maybe I can get all the dogs in the campground howling."

"You know what I'd like to hear."

I sigh. "What do you want from me, Braelynn?"

Her stare is hateful and I wonder what she'd say if I asked, if I begged her this very moment to marry me.

"I just want you to be reasonable. I want you to see reason."

"This coming from you? Is it reasonable to leave your date at concerts and family gatherings?"

"That was years ago! You're still holding that against me? Is that your excuse?"

"It's a long walk home from Wrigley Field."

"I came back but you wouldn't get in the car. That's on you."

"Why would marriage make you any different?"

The words and all their implications hang between us and I embark on an apology-fest that lasts until she tells me in very even and measured terms to go fuck myself. Then she vomits steak chunks and corn kernels into the glowing fire before stomping toward the tent. I call her back, but I know it's no use.

As the straps from the lawn chair dig into the back of my legs, leaving a tire tread pattern in my flesh, I realize that I may have put on a couple of pounds, slowed down just a little. It is a black night and the campground is quiet, mine the only fire still burning that I can see. I think about a S'more but don't have the gumption to fetch the ingredients from the car, tear into the packages, forage for a marshmallow stick. Brae would make a S'more even if she were alone. Brae is a firm believer in S'mores, and in my mind's eye I can see her breaking the crackers, rationing the chocolate, clasping small hands as they skewer fluffy marshmallows. I see her braiding her niece's hair, gently taming the knotted strands into silky rows, or playing Freeze Tag with Nicky and Kate, the foster kids next door, the girl hovering over her pyromaniac brother as he points his finger at me and shoots, gives me the evil eye. How could I *not* see this coming, not expect a woman who bakes brownies for the kids in the pediatric ward to want children of her own? I see Brae wiping kid's noses, bandaging knees and kissing foreheads. She would never leave her children at a sporting event, a roller rink, a birthday party; she wouldn't scold them in front of a waitress or snap at them for being playful. She would drive more safely with a child in the car.

I stare at the sky and name some new constellations: the Dragon's Claw, the Serpent's Fang, the Monkey's Tail. It occurs to me that I may be jealous of a child who's not even born. Am I ready to give Brae to a little person who will demand all of her time and energy, her love? Am I ready to share her with someone who will always come first? I think about my father, a distant, demanding man, his cold stare, his firm grip on my shoulder steering me in directions I never wanted to go, my mother soothing, coddling, turning against him in my defense. Could our child do this to us, become the dividing line in the before and after of our relationship? I think about Brae, making hot chocolate for her niece before they settle in to watch *Chitty Chitty Bang Bang* for the second time, forcing air into the neighbor boy's deflated bicycle tire with our rusted pump, frosting brownies with a plastic knife. I imagine her offering me one, pushing the frosting onto my nose and face, and the three of us laughing, Brae, me and our son in his grass-stained jeans, his large ears jutting from under a Chicago Cubs cap, or our daughter with her crooked teeth and her bright pink nail polish. It is a good life, the one I envision for us, the one I worry we will never have because I am afraid of so many things.

The fire has settled and even the lake is still, and I indulge the quiet until it becomes too quiet, until I imagine that while I mused the world swept past me and ended, the constellations above burned out and left behind their final iridescence, that I am alone in the universe and I can wish only one person back. I stare at the flap of the tent as if by willing it Brae will emerge, hug me or hit me with a wine bottle, command me to locate a stick while she rummages through the car for a flashlight.

"I am a S'more Slave!" I would shout.

"I am a S'more Master!" she would reply.

Instead I stare into the dark and imagine that my wish did not come true, that Brae is gone, and a chill descends. I snuff the fire and crawl into the tent, where Brae is snoring softly, cocooned in her four-season sleeping bag. When I place my arm around her shoulder and draw her close, she sighs dreamily in sleep.

The next morning, I fry bacon and eggs on the grill while Brae trudges off to the coin-operated camp showers. When she returns she says she isn't hungry, so I eat everything I cooked while she rolls her sleeping bag into a tight bunch and breaks down the tent after tossing my bag into a pile on the wet grass. Of course I should help, but team projects under these circumstances are emotional minefields so I keep my distance. By the time I finish washing the dishes and loading the gear, Brae is sitting in the passenger seat staring at the windshield. For a fleeting moment she looks like my father: steely eyes, set jaw, rigid shoulders, and I wonder if I am the one who brings out the worst in people.

When I pull toward the campground exit, I consider turning right instead of left, making a unilateral decision to head back east rather than continuing into unknown territory, but I realize that I don't want to be the one to give up, or at least be the one who is clearly to blame for our failed attempt at working things out. I make a left.

"I'm sorry," I say.

"For what?"

"For everything."

"What's everything?"

"I don't know. Insensitivity."

"Can you be more specific?"

Does she want me to list my infractions to prove that I understand what an asshole I am? "For saying what I did last night."

"Is that it?"

I draw a deep breath, clench the steering wheel in my fists.

"You don't love me enough," she says. "It's not even about marriage anymore. You just don't love me enough."

"What's enough?" I ask. "Isn't love *love*? Is there a meter or something? Why can't I just love you?"

She shakes her head. The conversation is officially over, both of us resigned, mired in that void of frustration and indecision.

We stop at a Country Kitchen in Utah for lunch and Brae stares through the plate glass window at the spectacle across the street: Peppermint Palace, a red and white explosion of brick and wooden architecture replete with a drawbridge and striped parapets stamped with trefoil designs.

Going against every instinct I have, I ask her if she wants to check it out.

"I could pick up some candy for the kids on the unit," she says, and the thought of the kids—even someone *else's* kids—makes her smile a little.

She scarfs down her turkey sandwich and I know her rush is not hunger from skipping breakfast but eagerness to get across the street and select gifts for kids who've lost their hair, their limbs, their will to live. Brae can be so mean yet so selfless; I can be so happy yet so scared. People are such contradictions that I wonder how anyone can survive a relationship for more than a week.

"Wow," I say as we enter the gatehouse to the Peppermint Palace, "I should have worn my sunglasses."

The inside walls are painted bright red and lined with shelves containing white candy in various shapes: canes, flowers, animals, suns and moons. As we enter the palace proper, walking onto a platform that encircles the entire inside of the building, I think of a circus: there are awestruck children staring and pointing at the massive candy production center below, while above us a red and white striped tent billows in a phantom breeze. Latex-gloved, white-hatted confectioners lean over slabs of candy on steel tables, instruments poised as if prepared for surgery, and taffy-pullers wind multicolored strands in large arcs, creating mosaic patterns on the canvas of wall behind them.

We make our way around the catwalk, children snaking between and around us as we press buttons attached to small speakers that describe the day's creations. The first recording is a pleasant voice telling us that we are watching the assembly of assorted Bubblegum Buddies. Today there are jungle-themed buddies in the shapes of zebras, tigers, elephants, and snakes, and when she hears this Brae nods as if the message is meant specifically for her.

Next, we're told about Lollipals, oversized suckers imprinted with whales, horses, butterflies, and fish, then Candy Climbers, which are peppermint sticks with marzipan animals in climbing positions attached. There are Twistpops, Chummy Chums, and Kookie Kakes, Circus Stix, Choco-Pals, and Bonzo Bars. Brae nods her way around the platform, and I watch her watch the production lines until I feel something small and moist in my hand, something wiggly and unfamiliar. I look down to see a little boy staring into the frenzy below, mesmerized, his hand in mine, clearly a case of mistaken identity. My first impulse is to shake him loose, but I just stand there waiting for him to notice and back away, frightened or embarrassed. He just gazes at the candy-filled conveyor belts, his fingers nestled comfortably in my palm. I've never held my father's hand that I recall, can't imagine sliding my fingers into his with such easy, unconscious grace. Brae looks at me, then at the boy, who must be around six years old, and she touches his head so gently that it makes me want to cry. Suddenly a woman screams out the boy's name, yanks his hand from mine, glares at Brae and me like we're criminals. What must it have looked like to her, her son holding a strange man's hand while his girlfriend stroked the boy's tiny head? The woman is trembling with worry or anger when she says she should call the police, refuses to listen when I try to explain, is still yelling when Brae pulls me by the arm to the gift shop, where she spends more than fifty dollars on cookies, gum, and taffy.

Afterward we climb into the car and I say, "You know I didn't do anything—"

"I know *that*," she says. "Fate is just against us. Everything we do is wrong." Then she bursts into tears.

Buying candy for sick children isn't wrong, I think, *taking a trip to work out our problems isn't wrong.*

"We're trying," I tell her. "That has to count for something."

"Are we?" she says. "Are we really trying?"

I don't respond and she says, "Let's just go home. You want to quit? Okay, I quit. I'm tired of being pathetic. I'm not going to beg you to marry me."

"I love you, but this isn't fair. Why is it marriage or nothing?"

"Because it just is."

We collapse into our own worlds as I head west on I-80 with a determination I can't quite place, perhaps a latent understanding that if I turn east I will lose her forever.

It is dark in so many ways when we cross the state line into Nevada. Brae's head is pitched sideways at an impossible angle and she is snoring into her left shoulder. What is she dreaming about? Us, our children, the indelible mark we'll leave upon this world, or maybe nothing at all, her mind one with the black, flat abyss through which we move at eighty miles an hour. We are in the desert, surely, so at first I think *mirage, hallucination.* But it is nighttime and I am not fevered or dehydrated. In the distance, rising up from the desert floor is a circle of wildly spinning lights, and I think *UFO*, which would seem a fitting end to our odyssey. As I move toward it I see a second circle of lights adjacent to the first, also flashing, casting multi-colored beams upward, endless spokes thrusting into the star-filled sky.

"Brae," I whisper, but she is now awake and staring at the spectacle ahead, clutching a bag of candy and smiling the smile of the rapt.

"It's a Ferris wheel," she says. "A double Ferris wheel. It's perfect," she whispers as she lifts a Kookie Kake to her lips.

We move toward that beacon in the desert as if hypnotized, seduced by the alien presence of light and chaos in an otherwise still and silent world. An hour later we are forking over thirty dollars for two unlimited ride bracelets.

"The park closes in an hour," says the gap-toothed girl in the tiny booth. "And these bands ain't good tomorrow."

"I am a wealthy poet!" I cry and wink at Brae.

She smirks and says, "I am a bank robber!"

We snatch the paper bracelets and run toward the midway. There is no line for the Antique Car ride so I usher Brae through the rope maze and she climbs into a green Model T. I enter the passenger side and slide next to her as she grasps the oversized steering wheel and slams her foot on the gas pedal repeatedly, jerking the car forward.

"Why didn't you get your own car?" she asks.

"I was afraid you'd crash into me."

She nudges me in the ribs but doesn't push me away or tell me to get out, so I put my arm around her as the car ricochets down the road.

"Wouldn't it be something if the car just kept going?" she asks, and I know exactly what she means. If we stayed in this car forever, moving in circles for eternity, we would never again argue about music, Brae would never have a child, I would never leave her.

The carnie at the Tilt-a-Whirl winks at us and points to car Number 8, and I know we'll think it's the fastest one even if it's not just because he recommended it. It's fast enough, and Brae laughs hysterically as our heads are pinned against the cart's metal grate, as I spin the large wheel before us and the cup-shaped ride careens around the undulating track.

We go on the Scrambler, Brae's body falling into mine with every spin, eliciting peals of laughter from her, and in the middle of the ride I conjure ways of taking her to an amusement park every day for the rest of our lives.

I see the Pirate Ship in the distance, a huge pendulum with long wooden seats like church pews, fake mast and rigging.

"Ahoy?" I ask. Brae hates this ride because she feels like she's going to fall out at the boat's upmost angle.

"What the hell," she says.

We are the only passengers, and the ride operator dares us to sit in the last row. Of course we do. "I am a sailor!" I cry. "I am a mermaid!" yells Brae. We sit in the middle of the bench and I put my arm around her waist and hold on tight. When the boat swings us backward toward the sky I tell her to close her eyes.

"I'll get dizzy, Jake," she argues.

"Trust me."

She closes her eyes, and I close mine, and we are sailing blindly, the wind whipping our hair, for the moment freed of gravity. It *is* dizzying, this loss of control, held aloft by an invisible force that swings us wildly forward and back, trapped again in a place where nothing matters but the physical sensation of our bodies responding to a strange and compelling momentum, to a course someone else has set. I enjoy this brief reprieve from the reality of our lives: the arguments, the fears, the impulsive decisions that steered us to where we are today and the unavoidable ones that will drive us forward later when the rides stop and the park lights go out. But for now, we are here, running like kids toward the Ring of Fire, where we hang upside-down in the rocking cart.

"I am a bat!" Brae cries.

"I am an oh-possum."

"A possum."

"I am Dracula," I say as I nuzzle her neck, the car swaying with the movement.

"I am a snake handler," she whispers, her fingers moving between my thighs and there we are, strapped into an amusement park ride in the desert, making out like oversexed teens.

The midway is vacant but for a few largely inert barkers, and we buy a huge cotton candy bush on a stick before moving toward the Haunted Mansion, a paint and plywood funhouse built entirely in a semi-trailer. Skulls and ghosts decorate the outside walls and spider webs dangle from the roof. We step onto the shaky aluminum stairs and into a dark corridor where Brae promptly bangs into a circus mirror. We stare into it and I want to say, "Here it is! A new angle!" but I look at Brae and see that she is staring solemnly at her mirror image; her head and legs are spaghetti-thin, but her belly is wide and round, encompassing the horizontal length of the mirror, and she caresses it gently. I step behind her, my head and legs a slim shadow behind hers, my ponderous belly an outline, and place my hand over hers as it moves in small circles across the great expanse of her girth. I kiss the back of her head and lean into her, our eyes meeting in the reflection.

She stares at me for a long time as if trying to read my mind, as if trying to see something new in this altered vision of me, this altered vision of us, different yet the same, old yet new, small yet expanding. I realize suddenly that she, too, is trying to make a decision.

"Braelynn?"

She closes her eyes and moves my hand across her belly, and in the mirror I see her holding a baby, then another, rocking them, smiling, placing her fingers on their downy heads as they grow into tow-haired children, toddlers in baseball jerseys, boys with dirt-smudged faces, boys with puppies and basketballs, boys with their heads buried under hoods of cars, boys in bathing suits, dress suits, men in tuxedos, men in sedans, men with babies in their arms, all staring back at Brae and me, standing there, right there, only a short distance behind us.

pocket philosophers

We were drinking over at the Apple Seed, me, Daly, and Jared, and Jared says he's hungry. So, Daly starts carrying on about Lucky Beef, how Pinky Tai's has the best damn Lucky Beef he *ever been exposed to*—that's an expression Daly uses more than I care to hear—how if he don't get some of that Lucky Beef yesterday he's going to cave in. By the time Daly's done with a visual and olfac-tree description of the Lucky Beef, Jared's passed out on the bar. I tell Daly it's late, but he does me like he always does and before long my sorry ass is behind the wheel of my rusted pickup. Daly throws Jared in the bed of the truck and we make our way up Pike and over the bridge into town. Sure enough, the place is closing just as we walk in smelling of whiskey and no good. This whisper of a Chinese woman says, "We close."

"Listen, sugar," Daly starts in real nice, "I just want—no, I *need*—some Lucky Beef."

"We close," she says.

"Do you know you got the prettiest eyes I ever saw?" he says, thinking he's a little smarter than he actually is.

She stares at him, and then a little Chinese man comes out of the kitchen.

"We close," he says.

"Are you the chef?" says Daly. "Because if you are, you're one kitchen magician. In fact, I don't believe I'll be able to sleep tonight if I don't get some of your Lucky Beef."

Telling this story makes me laugh, seeing as I'm looking at Daly right now and he's sleeping like a dead man, out cold from that head-on collision with the fish tank. Anyway, the man says we can get a take-out order and this cheers Daly up considerably 'til he says, "But no Lucky Beef."

Well Daly, who's prone to mood swings something awful, starts fussing. "So you won't give *me* any Lucky Beef?"

Now here's where I get worried because I know Daly; his voice changes, his back gets straight, it even looks like his hair's standing up. The little people stand there watching Daly's transfer-mation like it was nothing happening (though they ain't never seen his opening act, so how could they know?).

The man looks at Daly like he's cracked and says, "*No* Lucky Beef."

"Well, what if I just checked the kitchen?" says Daly, acting like the dang health inspector, and that's when I come in with reason, though that ain't never failed to fail before.

"C'mon, Daly. Let's just get some egg rolls." I turn to the straight-faced couple. "You got egg rolls?"

"How many?" says the woman.

"Nine," I say, but I just know after Daly's Lucky Beef speech at the Apple Seed he ain't gonna let it drop. The woman reaches for a pad to write down the order—she can remember it, sure, but these people are proud of their record-keeping—and Daly puts his mitt-sized hand over it.

"Now hold on a minute," he smiles. "I have this condition. I need Lucky Beef or I'll die."

The couple look at each other like they don't get it, but they stay still, though the woman 'pears to be getting frustrated.

"What if I said I'm not leaving 'til I *get* Lucky Beef?" says Daly like he got them by the short hairs.

Then something I never thought would have happened does, and it ain't the part about Daly testing the aquarium glass with his head neither. The little woman in her red and white dress and shiny slippers, her dark hair wrapped around sticks poking out the back of her head, her bony fingers on the edge of the order pad she can't budge because this idiotic lug's strong-arming her, starts screaming at Daly.

"You get out! No Beef! No egg roll! We close! You get out. I call the cops!" She reaches for the phone as the little man nods, but I can see he's scared, I can tell he wishes he'd brought along one of them Ginsu knives from the kitchen.

Right then I take a tally: no Lucky Beef, thirteen straight whiskeys and the fact that he was outdone by a little smidgen of a woman and wasn't a thing he could do about it (Daly's a fighter, but he ain't never hit a woman). So, he goes over to the fish tank real calm outside but bubbling over indoors and says, "Maybe I'll eat some fish then." The woman's yelling into the phone and she's excited; I'm betting they can't understand her but they'll be by soon enough.

Daly starts fiddling with the aquarium lid and I say, "Let's go, Daly. Now."

"Well, I'm still hungry," he says, "and if these folks won't give me some Lucky Beef"—and he starts drawing pitchers on the aquarium glass with his finger—"I'm gonna eat the big black one with the wings, and that one on the bottom with the whiskers."

"Po-lice coming," the little woman says. Actually, she sings it, her voice rising on the *ing* part. *That's* what helps it along, I'd say. Daly don't like being ignored or looking foolish, although he contributes plenty to making it happen, like just last month at the Saline Tavern when he fussed over that little mountain girl who wouldn't even look at him sideways. Maybe that's because her boyfriend, a skinny guy in a Carhartt jacket who'd been swilling Ole Smoky moonshine all night, was sitting on the barstool right next to her giving Daly the death scowl. This should have mattered to Daly, but it didn't. He bought her three Mai Tais—and she had no problem plucking out the red paper umbrellas and sucking them down, I can vouch for that—and then he recited some long poem about counting the ways he loved her or some such nonsense before her boyfriend finally had enough and waved a switchblade in his face.

"You're a flower," Daly said to her as he backed away from the pitiful jabs of Carhartt's knife.

"Let's go," I said to Daly, which is something I always seem to say to Daly.

"That bum ignored her all night," he said as he plopped down two barstools from the now drunken flower. "He didn't buy her a single drink!"

"Why's that your problem?"

"She can do better."

"We can all do better," I said, staring him down.

"Yes we can," he announced as if he hadn't just spent thirty minutes and twenty dollars on a girl who never said hello or thank you.

"Where's your pride?" I asked Daly, and I ask that same question as I go over to stop him from pulling at the aquarium cover he can't seem to budge. The little couple just stare at him–they must know something special about that lid because they don't even move.

Daly's steaming when he says, "If I can't eat some Lucky Beef I'm gonna eat some *un*lucky fish," which I think is pretty clever for a guy just had thirteen drinks. He's monkeying with that lid and doing such a bad job the fish don't even look scared. I know Daly, and I know just then he ain't thinking about Lucky Beef or Jared passed out in the truck or even the police coming to haul him off. All he's thinking about is getting that lid off. Anyway, he's coming unglued, banging on the top, looking at the sides for a secret latch or something, and then I see red and blue lights bouncing off the velvety wallpaper, streaking across the lanterns over the tables, even across Daly's face above that aquarium.

"Jesus Jude," I say to him, "you done me in tonight."

The woman runs to the front door to let in the cops and Daly stops and smiles. Right as Jed Jeffers, the judge's cross-eyed nephew just new on the force, plows into the restaurant in his overstuffed uniform, Daly slams his head full force into the aquarium. I hear the crack before I see what happened, and I ain't saying I believe in animal cruelty, but I was hoping it was the aquarium and not his skull that went. The glass cracked in a straight line the length of his forehead to his nose, and he went down like a lead sinker.

I get Jed to help me throw Daly into the bed of the truck next to Jared and I head for Lemmox County Regional, where I pull right up to the emergency doors. Two orderlies come running out with a stretcher as I unhitch the gate, and at first, they start pulling at Jared.

"No," I say, "the other one."

I have to help them haul Daly out the truck and struggle his six-foot, four-inch body onto the stretcher, and when I see his steel-toed boots hanging nearly down to the wheels, I gotta laugh.

"What about him?" one of them nods at Jared.

"He's just drunk," I say.

"And him?" he nods at Daly.

"Drunk *and* stupid," I say.

They tell me they're going to have to stitch him up, take X-rays, that it'll be a while. I look at the cherry-colored bloodstains on his work jacket.

"Okay," I say.

Jared's still snoring in the truck bed when I head for Daly's place, a defunct cider mill just outside Lemmox. I try to think about what he'll need—a toothbrush, clean underwear, some whiskey, his *Pocket Philosophers*, the one he's always quoting from. "Life is either a daring adventure or nothing, Wendall," he says to me.

As I drive up Old Mill Road, I start thinking about the first "daring adventure" I had with Daly and Jared at Spokes Roadhouse after Daly crotch-kicked a long-bearded biker who at the time happened to be surrounded by a small cluster of other long-bearded bikers. Daly saw him tap the eight-ball toward the corner pocket with his pinkie finger, so he stormed over and told him to put it back. The guy laughed in Daly's face, which you might guess turned red before Daly walked calmly around the leather-vested bear-man and moved the ball himself, making a show of lifting it in the air and slamming it down on the table in its original location. This is when the biker, who we now know as Victim Number Twelve, cracked Daly across the back of the head with a pool cue. Daly always fights fair until he's given a reason not to, so me and Jared knew that a boot and groin meeting was in the guy's immediate future. After Daly's size-thirteen Timberland slammed into Grizzly Adam's denim-covered nutcase, he, much like Daly in the Chinese restaurant, went down like a lead sinker. But that didn't stop his friends from launching a group effort to drag Daly outside and toss him headfirst into the windshield of a Jeep Grand Cherokee after swatting me and Jared off like flies. Here's the kicker: Daly wasn't even playing pool that night.

"Right is right," he'd said after we rolled him off the severely dented hood. "No one cheats on my watch."

"What do you mean, 'your watch'?" I asked, but when I saw Jared's eyes widen as he drew his finger across his neck, I let it drop. I later learned that Jared had heard, in countless forms, all of Daly's speeches—You Can Do Better, You Must Help Folks Grow, You Don't Cheat on My Watch—and at that moment he could not take one more.

It's plenty dark as my lone headlight shines up into thick stands of Scotch pine and dark spruce. The road is potholed something awful, and it's hard to see where I'm driving 'cause of my cockeyed beam. As I head uphill I start wondering if I latched the tailgate all right, if Jared ain't slipped out the back—I'd have a hell of a time finding him on this moonless night.

When I pull up to the mill, Trouble, Daly's boxer, bounds toward the pickup. She's already drooling when I reach for the glove box and get the rawhide, and she sits still while I fumble the key off her collar in the dark. Daly stole her from a lumberyard when she was just a pup, and he called her Trouble for the fun of it. He's always talking about how Trouble just follows him around, how he can't go too far without Trouble hunting him down, how he even sleeps with Trouble, and this gets the women who don't know any better feeling lowdown sorry for him. Well, the trouble with Trouble is she got beat up pretty bad by some guys at that yard. When Daly told me the story he went back and forth between fuming and heartbroken.

"Her eyes were swollen shut and she had broken ribs. Those who hurt the small and vulnerable will fester in the seventh circle of hell," he spat. "Poor little thing."

"Daly, hero of the downtrodden," I said, and he looked at me with such pride I never bothered to tell him I was joking.

But the memories have surely stayed with Trouble, who's jumpy as a cat in water around everyone but me and Daly and Jared. Old Man Warner come over once to pick up Daly's land survey—Daly leases his ten acres of apple trees to Warner, who combines it with his forty and sells to Mott's—and when he went to scratch Trouble's ear she near bit his hand off. That's when Daly started putting the key on her collar. This also keeps him from losing it when he's drunk.

"Go get Jared," I say to Trouble, and she jumps against the passenger window, the rawhide dangling from her mouth. Then she runs around back, looks into the bed of the truck and gives Jared up for dead before following me into the mill. I click on the light where Daly set up the kitchen—he eats on the counter where the last owner used to sell cider and smoked beef sticks—and, as usual, the place is spic 'n span. There's a woodburning stove in the center of the room, and I check the woodpile since I don't think Daly's gonna feel like chopping with a freight train riding in his skull, but he's more than caught up. He got a yellow note tacked up above the steel sink, something I ain't seen before, and it says in neat little letters: *Success is 99 percent failure*. "Amen," I say out loud, and Trouble gives out a little whine. You can't tell me she don't know Daly's gone and done something stupid again.

I grab a paper bag from under the sink and head for Daly's bookshelves. They're solid oak—Daly built them himself—about nine feet tall and the length of the south wall of the mill—forty feet, I'd say. My eyes get all crazy looking at some of those leather covers with the curlicue letters and, of course, I can't find *Pocket Philosophers*. He got books by a bunch of German fellas I don't care to spell out here, some foreign cookbooks, science fiction, and the smartest guy he *ever been exposed to*—Rousseau. I throw *The Social Contract* into the bag and head toward the metal Mustard, Smoked Cheese sign he left hanging over the bathroom. I toss his toothbrush in the bag and look for toothpaste but I can't find none. When I head for the closet, I see it on the window ledge next to the toilet: *Pocket Philosophers*. I add it to the bag, then grab some underwear, a flannel shirt, sweat socks, his Bricklayers 204 union jacket, and an army surplus blanket.

Back in the living room, which ain't a living room at all but a big open space in the center of the mill where the press used to be, I flop onto Daly's recliner and take a rest. Trouble flops down too, and by the sounds of it she's doing battle against that rawhide. On the end table I see the photo of Daly, me, and Jared standing in our waders holding up rainbow trout and smiling Olympic-scale stupid. My trout's the biggest, but that's only right since I introduced these fellas to the art of fishing. I'd just pulled into town—still had my beat-up couch and metal bed frame in back of the truck—and decided to stop at the first watering hole for whatever they had on tap. That was six years ago, and I can tell you, Daly and Jared was in a pathetic state of trout-fishing self-delusion back then. When I walked into the Apple Seed, Daly was lecturing on fly-tying. Every so often someone would say, "Is that so, Professor?" or "Smart boy like you ought to know." He was talking a blue streak where the facts weren't nearly as important as the delivery, and I could hardly keep still when he started in on the trout.

"You need a large, weighty fly with a flash of red." Here he touched the kerchief the barmaid had around her neck and I knew right off he was slick. "Trout need to see red if you want a good fight."

He seemed like a sociable, good-natured guy, so I said, "I think you're getting your trout and your bulls mixed up."

Daly looked at me, and it was then I realized he was about as big as a grizzly. "Excuse me?" he said.

"Well," I said, suddenly nervous as a blind man in a minefield, "trout don't care much about color. You can tag them with a red fly, a green fly, or a polka-dot fly, don't make them no never mind. They just want something *shaped* like food and *move* like food, the bigger the better."

I was almost finished with my beer but would have left the rest behind if that looked like the best course of action, and I thought about it when Daly got up from his barstool and headed over.

"Name's Daly," he said, "and that's Jared." He pointed to a fella who was holding onto the bar like it was a telephone pole in a hurricane. "We're trout-fishing tomorrow. Fall River. Interested?"

So that was that. We had a couple more beers and I told them about how the trout used to jump from the river, bounce two miles up a forest trail and then throw themselves at the kitchen window where my grandma used to tie flies. They helped me unload my stuff at the small A-frame my uncle left me and said they'd be by the next morning at five to pick me up. By five-o-one we were in Daly's van—me, Jared, Trouble, a case of Millers, a fifth of whiskey and some fancy sandwiches Daly made out of half-moon shaped rolls and chicken. Trouble snarled at me the whole way, even after Daly gave me two rawhides for making friends with, but after a couple of trout and some full-scale sniffing, she calmed down considerably. An old fella fishing downstream came over for a beer and Daly got him to snap our picture with his Sure Shot.

Other than a wooden plaque he bought at a resale shop in Ireland that translates to *Honesty Above All Else*, Daly's high school diploma's the only thing on the wall, and it amounts to this: Daly ain't really a professor, although that has never stopped him from professing. He got a knack for philosophy, and since he talks smart, people around here have taken to calling him Professor. They think he knows what-all about everything. "Professor, how'm I gonna get my tractor out the gulch?" and "What do you think of living in sin before marriage?" and "How do you get grease stains off upholstery?" I guess Daly's a damn good professor because he takes on every question without thinking too hard.

I give Trouble a few pats and clip the key back onto her collar. Jared's still snoring when I cover him up with the blanket, throw the paper bag onto the passenger seat and make my way back to town. It's about 4 a.m. when Jared knocks on the small window between the cab and the bed of the truck. When I open it he sticks his face in and says, "Where's the Lucky Beef?"

By the time we pull into the hospital lot Jared's laughing so hard he triggers a coughing jag and we got to wait in the truck for it to clear out—you don't go walking into no hospital acting like you got TB. Daly's still out when we get to the room he's sharing with some guy jumped out the window of his married girlfriend's bedroom and busted up his leg. I empty the bag into a little metal dresser next to Daly's bed and a big bruiser of a nurse with a cross 'round her neck comes in and starts manhandling his chart like it done smacked her around and run off with her best friend.

"How's he doing?" I say.

"How does it look?"

"Well," I say, "I ain't of the medical persuasion like yourself."

"I'd say he looks like he commanded a locomotive to stop, unsuccessfully," says Jared.

Daly split his face in half and it's stitched up the center. With his two bruised eyes it looks like he got a big old butterfly lying across his head.

"His blood alcohol level was point one-nine when he came in here." The nurse looks at us like she's studying a festering sore before stomping off.

Jared and me get some coffee from a machine in the hall and get to talking about the real culprit here, Lucky Beef.

"You know beef ain't their specialty," says Jared. "Their specialty's seafood."

"I don't see why they can't both be specialties."

He shakes his head like a man facing a river on a bicycle. "Because what they got is plenty a fish. They surrounded by the H-two-oh. They ain't got no room in China for cows to be running around. Hell, they hardly got room for themselves."

"Well, this ain't China."

"Folks stick with what they know. These people know how to fish and then how to cook it up. They ain't been cooking up cows back in the Mink Dynasty. They ain't learned that 'til they come to America, so how can they be any good at it?"

"It ain't that hard, Jared."

"Can you eat with chopsticks?"

"I ain't never tried."

"So, what do you take to more naturally, a fork and knife or some wooden sticks?"

"Well, the fork and knife only because I never learned—"

"That's right."

"But they can *learn* to cook cows just as good as shrimps."

"Will you ever take to the chopstick more than a fork and knife?"

"That's different."

He waves his hand across his face to wipe me from his sight. "This is only making me hungry," he says.

Three years ago when the Chinese folks opened up Pinky Tai's there was lots of conversations like the one Jared and I just had, some of them occurring right there in the restaurant. No one could figure out why anyone would open a Chinese restaurant in Lemmox, especially these folks dressed in clothes with dragons on them didn't speak no English. But eventually they got the farmers and their families, some tourists come out to fish, even us bricklayers to point to something on the menu had enough English in it to sound good. They were always running when we was in there eating chicken with the almonds or Moo Goo Guy in a Pan or even Lucky Beef. People in Lemmox generally got to liking Chinese food, and I'd have to say we were all on pretty good terms 'til Daly tried getting into that fish tank the hard way.

Back in the room I stare at Daly, his chapped lips, his bruised cheeks, the scar on his throat that crawls up toward his chin. I realize I can read Daly's history in his body: the neck scar from when he broke up a fight at the Rusted Crow, the crooked nose from its meeting with the fist of an amateur boxer he tried to stop from tearing up Stokie's after getting divorce papers, the face wounds and reddened knuckles from all the punches he took and gave after settling himself in the middle of other people's business, after riding their anger straight into his own.

Daly comes to just as Florence Nightingale finishes up with Hopalong next door, and she warns him not to sit up too quick.

"You're an angel of mercy," he says, touching his face about the center like he's taking a survey.

"Hmph," she says.

"So, what now?" Daly asks her.

"Observation," she says. "Doctor likes to keep head injuries around for a while, make sure they don't do anything strange."

"That doctor should have been around last night," Jared laughs, but the angel of mercy just squeaks out the room in them ghostly shoes.

"How's she look, boys?" Daly asks, pointing to his face.

"Prob'ly a little worse than she feels," says Jared.

"No matter," says Daly. "Mission accomplished."

Jared and me look at each other. Either Daly thinks he got some Lucky Beef last night, or he thinks he got into that tank.

"Well, Daly," I say, "the only mission you accomplished was to avoid getting arrested, and you went about that the hard way, if you ask me."

"Bah," says Daly, "I made a person last night. I'm Dr. Frankenstein."

"You sure look like it," Jared laughs.

"Not the monster," says Daly, "the guy who *made* him."

"They got you on some kind of medicine?" says Jared. "We brought along some whiskey'll shake it out."

Daly waves his hand across his face like Jared done earlier. "Did you see that woman come to life last night?" he says, smiling like an idiot. "You should have seen it, Jared."

Jared scratches his head.

"He's trying to say it was all *part of a plan*." I say it like I heard Daly say a million times before.

"Well," Daly laughs, "maybe one I didn't know about going in." He rubs the back of his head, squints and says, "But *everything* happens that way, you know. According to a plan. I'm just doing my part."

"Well, that don't make sense," I say, and open the *Pocket Philosophers*. "Look," I point to the words to back me up, "'it is characteristic of wisdom not to do desperate things.'"

"Well," says Daly, "define *desperate*."

"Aw, don't start *that* again," I say.

"Give it here." He yanks the book from my hand and flips directly to a worn, ruffled page. "Listen," he reads, "'it is the duty of the mind alone, not the mind and body together, to know the truth.' The body's not relevant here."

"You demonstrated *that* last night," I say.

"What I *demonstrated* is growth. Anyone can get mad. Hell, that's easy. But to get mad at the right person, at the right time, for the right reason, in the right way—that's *not* easy."

"You talking about you or her?" says Jared.

"She got mad as hell," says Daly, a small smile grabbing hold of his face. "She'll be better for it. She will. It's good to know what you're made of. That woman *grew* last night."

"So, you're saying you just got a lot uglier so some woman you don't even know can grow?" I say.

Daly shrugs. "What are bodies?" he asks as he slaps the book shut and stares at the cover. "Tiny envelopes that can't begin to hold the human spirit."

Me and Jared look at each other—we'd heard this envelope speech before.

"I'm too large for my envelope," says Daly. "My body's too small for my mind. Now and then I gotta break out."

Here we go, I think.

"Folks need to be shook up just to see what they're made of," says Daly. "The world needs to be shook up."

"Well, you're doing *your* fair share," says Jared.

"I cannot restrain my will."

"Maybe you ought to restrain your drinking."

Daly just laughs.

"You look tired," I say. "Whiskey in one of your sweat socks in the drawer if you need it."

"Thanks," says Daly.

"Need anything?" says Jared. "You want we should call Hogan?"

"I guess," Daly mumbles, the thought of Hogan probably ratcheting up the noise in his skull. "Look in on Trouble. There's chicken and livers in the fridge."

"Check," I say. "Anything else?"

Daly smiles and says, "Lucky Beef."

Jared and me make our way over to Pinky Tai's, and Jared goes in to ask if they got any Lucky Beef. Maybe the woman pairs him up with Daly and maybe she don't, but she says they ain't got no Lucky

Beef, disgusted-like, according to Jared. So I go in and ask how much it cost to fix the aquarium, or how much for a new one. Daly's good that way—he always pays for what he broke. The woman nods at the tank and I see they put some clear caulk over the crack—the glass is sweating some and there's a few drips on the carpet, but nothing to write home about. "Your friend nuts," she says to me.

"You're preaching to the choir," I say.

"We have no Lucky Beef."

"I'm getting that."

"How 'bout Sesame Beef, or Hoo-Nan Beef," says Jared. "He's so banged up he ain't likely to know the difference."

"Beef freezer broke," says the woman. "Chicken freezer okay, seafood freezer okay, beef freezer broke."

"The beef freezer done broke," says Jared. "No Lucky Beef."

You can imagine by then I was mighty tired of hearing *that*. "Well, what do you put in that Lucky Beef?" I ask.

She stares at me.

"You know, like mushrooms and peppers and what all. Like if I was to make it myself."

She thinks for a bit, then goes into the kitchen and leaves us standing there.

"She going to get a translator," says Jared.

"Ain't nobody in there speak English," I say.

Soon enough she comes out the kitchen with some plastic bags full of vegetables. "Here," she says as she shoves them at me, "five ninety-five."

I give her a ten and tell her to keep the change.

"You got ginger?" she says. "Sesame seed?"

I shrug.

She shakes her head and stomps off to the kitchen. She comes out with more plastic bags, smaller ones. I offer to pay and she pushes my hand away.

"Now the question's this," I say. "How'm I supposed to cook it up?"

She looks at Jared, then back at me.

"You know," I say, holding up the bags. "How do I turn this into Lucky Beef?"

She slams her hand on the counter. "No recipe!"

"Okay, okay," I say, nodding as I back out the door.

We drive to the Piggly Wiggly over in Truman to buy four big, lean Porterhouse steaks, and then we head for Daly's. Trouble's happy to see us, and she gets even happier when we throw her steak into a pan and it starts sizzling.

"All right," I tell Jared, "you cut that meat into strips look just like the ones at the restaurant, and I'll look through these books for directions."

He takes a carving knife and goes to it while I flip through the Chinese cookbooks for Lucky Beef, or at least its next of kin. It don't take long to find a dish that looks just like it, got the same vegetables and the sesame seeds and everything.

"Bingo," I say, and pull a large skillet off the rack. "Says here to use Chinese rice wine. He got any of that?"

Jared fishes through the cupboards. "Got some sherry. Daly'll like that."

"Okay," I say, "hand it over. And start smothering that beef with them seeds before I cook it up. Hold the fort on them vegetables," I say. "They go in last."

I flip Trouble's steak once and take it out the pan because she likes it rare. I cut it up and put it in the china bowl Daly gave her for her last birthday. At that moment, she's one happy pup. Jared got that meat climbing with seeds when I heat up the sherry and oil in the skillet to near smoking.

"Send 'er over," I say, and Jared starts laying the strips in the pan like they're dynamite sticks on a hot tin roof.

"We got to make some a that rice goes underneath," he says.

"Check," I say, and fish a box out the cupboard. The directions are pretty clear and I realize for the first time just how easy and relaxing cooking can be. I measure the water and rice and throw them in a pot, then I shift the meat around a little.

After we get the beef about half cooked up we start throwing in the mushrooms, peppers, spices, white disks the size of quarters, some sugar and vinegar, even some garlic Daly had. We lay on the soy sauce and let it cook a little. In the meantime, we eat some of the chicken and livers Daly got in the fridge so we won't be tempted to eat what we're making.

We open a couple a beers and Jared says, "We got to call Hogan."

"Tomorrow," I say. "Don't want to talk to the devil on Sunday."

"He's gonna flame."

"He can go to hell."

Hogan's our foreman at the Brentwood Estates we're building over in Easton County for rich folks don't know what to do with their money. Daly actually got both me and Jared our jobs—got me on as apprentice bricklayer, Jared already knew what he was doing going in—because he's the union steward and he got say in such matters. I'm thinking about just the same thing when Jared says, "Think he's still steamed about McCory?" That happens a lot, us thinking the same.

"If it ain't McCory it's someone else he's hot for," I say. "Hogan's always thinking about someone."

We were on overtime Saturday morning putting the final shakes on a foundation when McCory, a new kid on the job Hogan been riding like a mule, runs a CAT into the east wall of the house we just finished next door and Hogan flies off like a man from a cannon.

"You stupid son-of-a-bitch," he yells at McCory, who's sitting on that CAT with his mouth open, looking as if someone else just hit that wall. "Back it out," Hogan yells, but McCory's so shook up he forgets to put it in reverse and smacks the wall again. Then Hogan's up on that CAT pulling him off by the shirt. Daly gets a gander and he's between 'em before I can pray for assistance.

"You're fired," Hogan screams at McCory, and it's all the kid can do to keep from crying. Then Hogan stomps off and Daly stomps after him.

"Hold on," says Daly, all red in the face and looking like he needs to kill something. "You just hold on."

Hogan stops walking, turns to face Daly, and I ain't never sure when this stuff happens if Hogan listens because he's scared of Daly or because Daly's the union steward or both.

"You're not going to fire that man," says Daly, pointing to McCory, who's standing off to the side sniffling. "He's still in training. He messed up because you been pushing him to do the work of three guys since he started." Daly gets up close to Hogan, puts his finger near Hogan's eye and says, "It's *your* fault he hit that wall."

"I can't afford mistakes," yells Hogan. "*His* mistakes. He's gone."

"All right then. C'mon, fellas," says Daly, waving his arm across the site as if to sweep us all up.

Jared drops a spade full of cement and climbs over the foundation wall, then Sam and Chevron wipe their hands on their aprons and leave the cement mixer, and Max and Ripperton climb down off their CATs and start walking too. I take off my gloves and hard hat and set 'em on the ground.

"What do you think you're doing?" yells Hogan. "What the *hell* do you think you're doing? We're staring down a deadline here."

"You take McCory back, we all come back," says Daly. "You fire him and we all walk."

Daly's the best damn bricklayer in the county, maybe even the state, hell, maybe even the world, so Hogan knows what he's losing. Of course, Daly's always up Hogan's ass like a flaming hemorrhoid, so Hogan knows what he's keeping too.

"All right," says Hogan, all red in the face, "but no one leaves 'til that wall is fixed, and I'm not paying anyone past six."

"Fair enough," says Daly, because he saw what I did two seconds after McCory hit the wall—that there was only surface damage. We could grind it down, replace a few bricks. "Something else," says Daly, and here Hogan starts steaming because he knows Daly don't give something for nothing.

"What!" yells Hogan, wiping his forehead with a stiff hand.

"We're *all* working towards improvement, not perfection," says Daly. "Every man here gets respect. You touch one of these guys again, there's gonna be hell to pay." Daly's shaking mad, almost as if he hates Hogan even more for backing down, for not hitting him, for not giving Daly an excuse to break out of his envelope.

Hogan nods and stomps off toward the trailer, and Daly tells McCory to grab a spade and work alongside Jared. "Wendall," he says to me, "let's you and me fix that wall. Let's set a record."

We finish the wall and the foundation before six, and that makes Hogan none too happy, so we're feeling like we just won the war when we get to the Apple Seed and settle in for a few drinks. Thirteen whiskeys later Jared starts whining about being hungry, and you know the rest. Looking back, maybe Daly was still mad at Hogan when he crashed into that aquarium.

"Hogan ain't mad at McCory," says Jared as he stirs the Lucky Beef. "He's mad at Daly but ain't a thing he can do about it but pick on the men. That's how he gets to Daly."

"Someday Daly's gonna kill him."

"Ain't a man on the site turn him in."

The whole mill smells of ginger and garlic when we scoop the Lucky Beef into a plastic bowl and the rice into another one. When we get to the hospital Daly's awake, and the angel of mercy tells us the doctor gave him near a double dose of pain killers but it didn't knock him out.

"You look like hell," Daly says to me, and I realize I ain't slept in two days.

"Well, you're the authority on *that*," I say.

Jared takes the bowls out the bag, then sets them on Daly's tray.

"You got your rice and you got your Lucky Beef," he says as if Daly's blind.

Daly stares at the bowls like they're full of diamonds. "Where did you get it?"

Jared starts in on a ten-hour story and I interrupt. "It wasn't no trouble," I say. "We cooked it up real easy and we can do it again whenever we want. I don't expect that at the present we're welcome at Pinky Tai's anyway."

"Do not content yourselves with the opinions of others," Daly says as if we're the ones just tried to poke our heads through a glass wall without the aid of equipment.

Daly's eating so fast the sparks are flying from his utensils. "This is the best Lucky Beef I ever been exposed to," he says, and Jared says *Thank you* like I was a piece of dust in the whole matter. Daly stops eating, looks at us and says, "You fellas have the souls of saints, do you know that?"

Well, I don't see myself as no saint, and I sure don't see Jared as one, so I let it drop and blame it on the medication. He sees he made us uncomfortable, so he changes the subject.

"Call Hogan?" he says.

"Yep," I answer without looking at Jared. "Said you had an accident and he said accidents happen. Get back when you can."

Daly don't appear to be surprised by this, but that could also be the pills playing with him. "You tell him I'll be back before anyone expects me," he says. "That'll keep him on ice."

I stare at Daly's bruised and broken body and decide to ask something I been wanting to for years, thinking maybe the drugs'll make him honest. "Daly," I say, "you trying to kill yourself?"

He puts down his fork and knife real slow, pushes his plate away and stares at me. "Is that what you think?"

Jared looks at the floor and I realize he's been thinking the same thing.

"Seems mighty coincidental, you putting yourself in per-carious situations," I say. "Fighting, carrying on, slamming your head into solid objects. Do you want to die? Because if you do, I can arrange it nice and neat. I ain't gonna watch you kill yourself inch by inch."

Daly laughs, but there's tears in his eyes and I'm sorry I asked.

"I like living more than dying," he says. "I do a little of each every day, but the scale's still tipped to the living side."

He starts eating again, but now Jared takes on.

"I ain't saying it does a good job or nothing, I agree with you there," he says, "but you still need your envelope, Daly. You gotta stop."

"I have a responsibility to society."

"What about your responsibility to yourself?" I say.

"And to us?" says Jared, which comes as a surprise because I been thinking the same thing.

"You are my brothers," says Daly, and he starts blubbering to beat the band. This'll be our secret forever because it wasn't Daly crying at all but the painkillers acting on him. Then he says, "But know that if you want to change things, you *have* to catch the eye of the world, you *have* to make a fuss."

"Well goddammit," I say, "we're just going to have to find a better way to make a fuss." I grab the *Pocket Philosophers* from his bedside table and flip through. "Here: 'It is *not* enough to have a good mind; the main thing is to use it well.' You—"

"They didn't have no Lucky Beef," Jared interrupts.

Daly stares at him as if the words are flying around his brain looking for a place to land.

"That's right," Jared says, shrugging. "They weren't holding back, they just didn't have any."

"But you get mad before you even ask," I say. "You're always ready to fight even when there's nothing to fight about."

Daly is quiet for a long time, his fist curled into a tight knot as he stares through swollen eyes at himself in the metal tray, the soy sauce on his chin, the stitches inching up his face like a tiny railroad track. Even the angel of mercy, who storms into the room with a sour expression, backs out quietly when she sees the look on Daly's face, a cross between wonder and grief. "Well," he finally whispers, "I am indeed amazed when I consider how weak my mind is . . . and how prone to error."

Daly leans back on his pillow, closes his eyes, moves his hand up and down his face, tracing the wiry sutures with his fingertips. He then places both hands over his belly like a dead man, and after an eternity goes by and we think he's fallen asleep, he sighs.

"Yes," he says into the air where maybe he sees Sartre and Rousseau, or the whiskered biker or the Chinese woman, or even Hogan himself. "Yes. We are going to find a better way to make a fuss."

harm none

Nancy dropped the phone into its cradle and glanced through the bay window overlooking the herb garden. Maeve, stooped in the second-to-last row of plants, picked savagely at the yarrow flowers, her eighty-year-old hands dropping them into a small wicker basket with incredible precision. Nancy waved both arms above her head, but Maeve continued to move methodically down the line, glancing occasionally toward the clouds and silently cursing the overcast sky. *Stubborn woman*, Nancy thought. She opened the French doors when the rain began and watched Maeve tap the basket to shake off the droplets before entering.

Maeve crumbled the yarrow leaves into a pot of water Nancy had set to boiling when Gadling called to say he'd split his lip again. By the time he arrived with a half loaf of sourdough pressed to his mouth, Maeve had strained the yarrow in cheesecloth and flattened the mixture between her palms. She yanked the bloodied bread from his hand and pushed the poultice to his lip. The bleeding stopped even before he sat down.

"Achillea millefolium," said Maeve.

"Ah," Gadling managed, faking interest.

"Named for Achilles, who is said to have used yarrow to heal battle injuries in the Trojan War."

"Huh."

"How's that feel?" asked Nancy.

Gadling removed the poultice slowly, used Nancy as a mirror.

"It's all stopped," she said, then turned to Maeve. "Speaking of stopped, Pem just called. She needs dandelion."

"There's a sack of potatoes on the landing," said Gadling as he rose to leave. "You're a gem."

"Obliged," said Maeve.

Gadling left and Nancy stared at Maeve. "What about Pem?"

"Tomorrow. A day's discomfort will be a diet lesson."

"What if she calls back? She's frantic."

"Tell her I'm in the garden. Or at the market. Or on the moon. I don't care what you tell her. She won't get dandelion today."

Nancy did not understand Maeve's selective benevolence. Gadling was a klutz who regularly hacked up his feet with axes and cracked into wooden doors, yet Maeve never denied him immediate help. But Pem, a good-natured woman with a lifelong weight problem, suffered because Maeve had seen her eating Cheetos at her sixtieth birthday party, her double-wide splattered with banners, balloons, and tables laden with grease-soaked nibbles: potato chips, snack cakes, crullers, pork rinds.

"Maybe it was stress eating," Nancy had suggested. "She was so upset when her nephew's girlfriend stormed out of the party and left him behind. You remember that girl, Caelynn or Brandalyn or something."

Maeve ignored her so she tried another tack. "Or maybe she was celebrating, just this once."

"Well," said Maeve, "it's her intestines that're dancing now, and with cheese as the doorman, nothing will be leaving *that* party."

Maeve, as if reading her mind, told Nancy to relax. "Have some chamomile tea," she said. "And remember that we practice *holistic* healing."

Nancy was Maeve's daughter-in-law, married to an only child who disappeared in Vietnam. She had moved in with Maeve when Josh was drafted and stayed on through the Battle of Xuan Loc, the treaty at Paris and the delivery of a telegram with the letters MIA typed neatly inside. Nancy and Josh had planned to buy a small farm just up the road from the recently widowed Maeve when he returned, grow corn and alfalfa, maybe raise some chickens. The owner of the farm waited right along with Maeve and Nancy for Josh to come home, held on for five years until his health failed and he, along with the U.S. government, gave Josh up for dead and sold the farm to a real estate developer. Nancy promised Maeve the day the telegram arrived that she would stay until Josh came home and, although she did not count herself superstitious, she felt her leaving would forever seal the small door in the universe through which he might someday return. Decades later, the women seldom spoke of Vietnam, although a tangible reminder in the form of a yellowed telegram remained on the mantle propped between two tarnished candlesticks.

Maeve visited Pem the following day with a tea mixture of dandelion, yellow dock root, and licorice.

"Thank God," said Pem, who was bent over her sofa, a floral muumuu rippling at her swollen feet in the breeze sent by a small floor fan.

"Only one cup before meals," warned Maeve. "Any more and you'll grow immune."

Maeve handed Pem a cup and sat self-consciously on a wicker fan chair, the only seat in the room other than on the already overtaxed sofa beside Pem.

"Thanks for bringing it," said Pem. "I'm so cramped I can hardly walk."

"One cup," said Maeve. "If it doesn't work we'll have to try ispaghula husks and slippery elm."

"I'll try anything."

"You can't eat on that remedy."

"Nothing?"

Maeve shook her head.

"Let's try this for now," said Pem.

"Call me if you need," said Maeve as she rose awkwardly from the unwieldy chair. "And drink lots of water." Maeve brushed Pem's shoulder gently as she passed, visualizing an electric current pulsing from her fingertips straight to Pem's intestines like a roto-rooting lightning bolt.

Maeve had learned to cultivate herbs as a child, spending long hours in her grandmother's garden rubbing basil between her fingertips and snipping the heads off pot marigold for one of her grandmother's tinctures. She had helped cure Auntie Ann's sties and Mr. Whit's rheumatism, and even though her mother had said it was all poppycock, she felt the power of the herbs when she lay in bed at night chewing peppermint or sniffing the dried lavender she had stuffed into her pillow. When her grandmother died at the age of ninety-four, Maeve, quietly and through no conscious effort, assumed her role as local herbalist. Ambridge had a town doctor, of course, but unless a heart valve was slapping shut or a limb was split in two, most folks turned to Maeve, who practiced preventive medicine. The doctor was a young man recently graduated from medical school who visited Maeve shortly after his arrival to say that he appreciated all she did to make his job easier. He didn't care if the effects of her herbal remedies were psychosomatic or otherwise; he only cared that they often appeared to work.

Maeve once thought she'd need the town doctor to deliver her grandchildren. She had expected Josh to return from the war and fill Nancy, who at the time Maeve viewed simply as a waiting receptacle, with seeds enough from which to choose an heir—a scrawny, introverted waif of a child with a mind for hard thinking and an intuitive bond with the land. In the absence of a grandchild Maeve attempted to teach Nancy, who had certainly possessed the intelligence and the desire to learn but lacked the discretion required to firmly minister to the emotional as well as physical ailments of her charges. Nancy always peppered her advice with maternal concern

("Aw, honey, it'll be all right with a little spikenard rubbed in" or "three drops of valerian in your raspberry tea'll kill those cramps right off, doll"), creating emotional dependence that disempowered them. She could not seem to grasp that herbs and the will of the healer merely stimulated the natural, self-healing energies of the patient, that energy sent to sick people did not replace their responsibility for their own well-being but simply kicked their own healing into gear.

Even so, Nancy had learned the names and properties of each of the seventy herbs in Maeve's gardens in several weeks, and she had developed a facility to divine precisely where to seed new plants so that they prospered. When the women had difficulty meeting monthly bills, it was Nancy who hatched a plan to save the farm: they would open the lovely gardens to the public. After all, weren't there always tourists coming around to see the old battle sites, the museums, the whales? They could offer classes on herb cultivation and host small afternoon lunches during which they would serve homemade herbal teas and edible wildflower salads with stone-baked bread. Maeve liked the idea when she realized that the gardens and classes would be filled with potential heirs, and she was suddenly proud of her daughter-in-law's ingenuity.

The women propped a sign against the front gate advertising lunches with limited seating in a restored farmhouse, and their first guests were four elderly widows who'd leased a van to "chase down America," according to the one with the clacking dentures.

"Plymouth Rock and witch trials," said the one with the ill-fitting wig, "now *that's* America." The others nodded and sipped their marshmallow and wild lettuce tea.

"This is wonderful," said the Clacker. "I feel . . . relaxed."

"Wild lettuce was once sold as a substitute for opium," said Maeve as she placed a tray with raspberry-hazelnut scones onto the table. "The tea calms."

"Do you sell it?" asked the Wig.

"Of course," said Nancy, who immediately went to the kitchen to measure and crush the dried mixture into a baggie tied with curled ribbons.

Maeve and Nancy decided to package and sell the teas after this successful luncheon, during which the guests happily crunched their way through alfalfa sprout and cream dill finger sandwiches, berry scones with homemade rosehip jam and an elderflower and hyssop salad with lemon pepper dressing. There was a small scare when the Clacker hooked her dentures into a tough lavender stem and pulled them halfway out of her mouth, but the relief with which she recovered herself was epidemic, and the geriatric explorers left promising to sing the praises of the tea farm to the entire country during their travels.

Nancy used the proceeds from the first lunch to order a custom sign for the new business from Gadling, the best woodcarver in the county when he kept his mind on his work.

"A roughhewn maple log with the words 'Harm None' carved into it. And two hooks for hanging it between the poles on the front porch."

"Harm None?" said Gadling.

"Just make it," said Nancy. "And try not to hurt yourself," she laughed. "It's a surprise for Maeve."

Two weeks later when Gadling pulled up to the farmhouse with the sign in the back of his rusted Silverado, Maeve rushed to the kitchen to ready a poultice for him until she heard Nancy's ecstatic chirping.

"Look!" she squeaked, pointing through the screen door at Gadling, who held the log in his meaty arms.

For a moment Maeve thought she was hallucinating. She didn't understand what Gadling was doing on her porch holding a log inscribed with her grandmother's parting words, but she finally understood that Nancy had not only remembered but wanted to immortalize the chief doctrine of all true herbalists.

"It's lovely," said Maeve.

"It's for the tea farm," said Nancy. "It's the name of our new business."

Maeve did not understand how those words would entice prospective customers, but the sign *was* beautifully carved and she didn't always go in for logic herself. "Well," she said, "it *is* lovely."

Word of the unique fare at Harm None spread quickly, and soon lunches were offered by reservation only. Classes were almost always full of tourists who had enjoyed the food and the sense of well-being inspired by the farm's rolling gardens, eco-conscious young couples bent on saving both money and the planet, and locals who had always been curious about Maeve and her mythical herbs. They took notes when she said that vervain was regarded as sacred by the Druids because of its magical properties, that mint will overtake a garden if not curtailed by metal walls sunk deep into the earth, that garlic and cayenne are natural pest control alternatives.

The Chamber of Commerce added Harm None to its list of attractions, and soon the women planted theme gardens. The Shakespeare Garden featured herbs mentioned in the bard's plays—wormwood, mustard seed, marjoram, larkspur and wortsbane—and the Biblical Garden contained varieties of sage, thyme, rosemary, Lady's bedstraw, and pennyroyal. The Medieval Monastery Garden included vegetables, fruits, flowers, and culinary and medicinal herbs of the Middle Ages. Guests were encouraged to meditate among the fragrant blooms of lamb's ear, heliotrope, and calendula.

Visitors were allowed to roam all of the gardens except the one Maeve tended with most care: Josh's garden, planted on a hillside far from the house in a large patch of fertile, sun-dappled soil the day the telegram arrived. In it she grew oregano, coriander and chives, the herbs Josh favored growing up. Maeve, like Nancy, felt it was certainly possible that Josh was alive, and she refused to kill that possibility by believing him dead. So Nancy had stayed on at the farm and Maeve had planted seeds on a bright hill in a heart-shaped garden.

People couldn't get enough of the gardens and their bounty. The women grew, harvested, dried, canned, and packaged ingredients for the garlic-dill and tarragon vinegars, apple rosemary and pineapple sage jellies, peach and plum chutneys and a variety of herbal teas and dried flower sachets they sold. The lunch menu and the clientele grew until Maeve worried she would be unable to help run the business and minister properly to the people in her care. It was ultimately decided that luncheons and classes would be conducted only twice a week barring special requests from sincere out-of-towners while the "shop" would remain open all week. As if on cue, the telephone rang the moment the new, less demanding schedule had been set.

"It's Pem," said Nancy, her hand covering the mouthpiece. "She says she needs ispaghula husks and slippery elm. She's desperate."

"Tell her I'm coming," said Maeve, who collected several dried herbs, roots and seeds into a satchel and motioned Nancy to the door. "Drive me," she said.

When they arrived at Pem's, Maeve prepared a decoction of slippery elm and fresh ginger root and a bowl of Raisin Bran topped with ispaghula husks.

"Eat it," said Maeve, "and eat only that until you're cleared. Anything else you eat will impede you."

"Trust me. I won't eat a thing," said Pem, who grimaced as the husks popped between her teeth.

"They'll hurt even more coming out," said Maeve, "but you've let it go too long. Why didn't you call sooner?"

Print flowers rippled across her chest as Pem shrugged her massive shoulders, and Nancy discreetly motioned Maeve toward the kitchen.

"We'll get you some water and a cold cloth, hon," Nancy said to Pem. "Sit tight." She regretted the words immediately. "Geez," said Nancy, "I'm always saying the wrong things."

In the kitchen, Nancy ran a dishrag under the faucet, then pointed to the top of the refrigerator at a haphazard pile of snack cakes, cheese crackers, gummy bears, and popcorn. "I thought about throwing them away. Then I realized how ridiculous that was. How everything I do is ridiculous. Thinking I can cure people with talk, that I can throw away their temptation." She filled a jelly glass with cold water, plopped in two ice cubes and turned to Maeve. "Even thinking for so long that Josh would come home."

Nancy marched from the kitchen and back to the living room, placing the cold compress on Pem's forehead. "Here you go, Sweets," she said, handing over the ice water. "Drink up."

As Nancy drove home that night, Maeve stared at the windshield. "You can't cure people with talk alone or rid them of temptation, that's for sure," she said. "But you do help them plenty. I don't want to hear you talking that nonsense anymore."

"But I'm—"

"What's more," said Maeve, "Josh could still come home."

Pem called the next day to say that the husks had worked.

"The tonic of the Titans," said Maeve.

"What's that?"

"Nothing."

"I was thinking," said Pem, "of going on a diet. Maybe talking to Dr. Rosen."

"I think that's a fine idea."

"It was Nancy's. She said she'd go with me."

"Well," said Maeve, "I think that's fine too."

Later that afternoon Maeve joined Nancy in the garden and the two women weeded the burdock before moving on to the flower gardens.

"Pem says you're taking her to the doctor," Maeve said as she snipped a daisy from its willowy stalk.

"I just thought . . . she needs—"

"It's good. It's *very* good," said Maeve as she handed the flower to Nancy, a peace offering, a baton, a torch.

The following day there would be twelve guests for tea biscuits with blueberry syrup, dandelion and plantain salad with cinnamon-raspberry sauce and lemon balm cake with meadowsweet and burdock tea. The women gathered the ingredients and moved toward the porch, where a deeply carved log swayed lightly in a breeze swept from a hill far above the house where the sun cradled a lush herb garden.

acknowledgments

Every published book is a group endeavor. I am much indebted to the team at Baobab Press—Christine, Danilo, Margaret and Casey—for their vision, expertise, and encouragement, and for offering my book a perfect home. I owe special thanks to a group of talented, generous writers for their close reads, keen insight, and constant encouragement: Yes, I'm talking to *you*. Thanks also to the Detroit Writers' Guild for hosting fine readings and to all of the inspiring members of Detroit Working Writers. As always, I'd like to thank my students for being such fine readers and writers.

about the author

Dorene O'Brien is a Detroit-based writer and teacher whose stories have won the *Red Rock Review* Mark Twain Award for Short Fiction, the *Chicago Tribune* Nelson Algren Award, the *New Millennium Writings* Fiction Prize, and the international Bridport Prize. She has earned fellowships from the NEA and the Vermont Studio Center. Her stories have been nominated for two Pushcart prizes, have been published in special Kindle editions and have appeared in *The Best of* Carve *Magazine*. Her work also appears in *Madison Review, Short Story Review, The Republic of Letters, Southern Humanities Review, Detroit Noir, Montreal Review, Passages North, Baltimore Review, Cimarron Review,* and others. *Voices of the Lost and Found*, her first fiction collection, was a finalist for the Drake Emerging Writer Award and won the USA Best Book Award for Short Fiction.

The body of *What It Might Feel Like to Hope* is set in Garamond, an old-style serif typeface created by sixteenth-century Parisian engraver Claude Garamont.

The cover headers of *What It Might Feel Like to Hope* are set in Trajan Pro 3, a display serif typeface released in 1989 and developed by Carol Twombly and Robert Slimbach for Adobe.